RIDERS OF THE BUFFALO GRASS

Bliss Lomax was a pseudonym for **Harry Sinclair Drago**, born in 1888 in Toledo, Ohio. Drago quit Toledo University to become a reporter for the Toledo *Bee*. He later turned to writing fiction with *Suzanna: A Romance Of Early California*, published by Macauley in 1922. In 1927 he was in Hollywood, writing screenplays for Tom Mix and Buck Jones. In 1932 he went East, settling in White Plains, New York, where he concentrated on writing Western fiction for the magazine market, above all for Street & Smith's *Western Story Magazine*, to which he had contributed fiction as early as 1922. Many of his novels, written under the pseudonyms Bliss Lomax and Will Ermine, were serialised prior to book publication in magazines. Some of the best of these were also made into films. The Bliss Lomax titles *Colt Comrades* (Doubleday, Doran, 1939) and *The Leather Burners* (Doubleday, Doran, 1940) were filmed as superior entries in the Hopalong Cassidy series with William Boyd, *Colt Comrades* (United Artists, 1943) and *Leather Burners* (United Artists, 1943). At his best Drago wrote Western stories that are tightly plotted with engaging characters, and often it is suspense that comprises their pulse and dramatic pacing.

RIDERS OF THE BUFFALO GRASS

Bliss Lomax

First published in the UK by Collins

This hardback edition 2012
by AudioGO Ltd
by arrangement with
Golden West Literary Agency

ISBN 978 1 458 8723 4

British Library Cataloguing in Publication Data available.

Printed and bound in Great Britain by
MPG Books Group Limited

CHAPTER ONE

THE DENVER AND PACIFIC'S Western States Express had been held up for better than forty minutes, in Salt Lake City, waiting for Tom Moran's private car to be coupled on.

The Utah countryside, shimmering in the bright morning sunshine, received scant attention from Moran, the road's general manager, and the four men seated with him in the comfortable lounge as the train sped northward to Ogden. Though the trouble that confronted them was three hundred miles away on the Snake River Plains of southern Idaho, it was responsible for this hurriedly called conference.

"You haven't given Ripley and his partner much time to reach Ogden, Tom," one of the four observed, tossing aside the timetable he had been studying. "There's only one train they could catch that would get them there."

The speaker was a trim, precise little man, with graying hair, who long had been a big wheelhorse in the affairs of the D. and P. His official title was Assistant to the President, an honor that had not come of his seeking; had it been left to him, little Ambrose MacDonald would have preferred to remain anonymous, letting his labors for the company speak for themselves.

"They'll be there," Moran assured him confidently. "In my wire, I told them the matter was urgent." He chuckled pleasantly. "I know that pair; it doesn't take them long to get moving. And they'll do a job for us. I used them three or four times when I was running the Rocky Mountain Shortline. They never failed to come through for us." He turned to his Chief of Detectives. "Pat can bear me out on that."

Pat Garner nodded. "They'll finish what they start,' he said thinly.

Across the way from him, Dan McCandless, head of

construction for the Denver and Pacific, shook his head pessimistically as he pulled himself up in his chair. "They may be all right, but they're a couple range detectives—ex-cowboys. If we had some rustlers to chase, they might be okay."

"Don't let that cowboy angle throw you, Mac," Moran declared sharply. "They're cowboys—and proud of it—but they haven't trailed a rustler in years; they go after bigger game than that. They've worked for Wells Fargo, the Aztec Copper Company, and I don't know how many banks and railroads. I know they can handle this job; the only question in my mind is whether they'll agree to take the case. If they do, it will be as a personal favor to me."

"You're a hundred-percent right," little Ambrose MacDonald agreed. "I haven't forgotten the licking they handed the D. and P. a couple years ago when I tried to grab the narrow-gauge Thunder River and Northern for nothing." Ambrose sighed regretfully. "They made us pay through the nose for that piece of rusted junk. It'll be some comfort to know that if they get mixed up in this business in Idaho that they'll be on our side of the fence."

Though he would have been the last to say so, he knew as well as Moran and the others in the car that acquiring the Thunder River and Northern had been the making of the D. and P. "Rusted junk" accurately described the little road's rolling stock; but its right of way down Thunder River Canyon was priceless. It had enabled the Denver and Pacific to straighten out its east-west mainline, with a net saving of two hundred mountain miles between Denver and Salt Lake City and giving it such an advantage over its competing roads that before the bubbling cauldron of railroad-financing and horse-trading cooled off, the D. and P. had gobbled up the Rocky Mountain Shortline and forced a merger on a far western road that took it all the way to the Coast. Shortly thereafter, the now familiar slogan "The Thunder River Route" began to appear in the D. and P.'s advertising and on its rolling stock—an idea born in Ambrose MacDonald's fertile mind.

The short run to Ogden did not take long. Out in the

yards, Moran's car was cut off and pushed onto a siding. As usual, he had his long-time secretary, Gene Dunnigan, with him. "Gene," he said, "you know the boys; run up to the depot and see if you can locate them."

Dunnigan had been gone only a few minutes when he was seen returning, accompanied by a tall young six-footer and a grizzled, pint-size little man.

"It's Rainbow Ripley and Grumpy Gibbs," Moran exclaimed. Speaking to McCandless, he added, "The tall, lean-faced one is Ripley, Dan."

Only McCandless had to be introduced to the partners. This was the first time, however, that they had encountered Ambrose MacDonald since the bitter fight over the Thunder River and Northern. But they bore him no ill will; and he, for his part, greeted them affably, saying, "We meet under pleasanter circumstances than the last time, gentlemen. I used to lie awake, wondering where you were going to hit me next."

"By grab, you gave us some sleepless nights, too," Grumpy declared good-naturedly. "It was a little rough, wasn't it, Rip?"

"I seem to remember that it was," Rainbow acknowledged, his gray eyes narrowing in a crinkly smile. "We just happened to be in town when your wire reached us," he continued, addressing Moran. "Fortunately, our range clothes and riding-gear were still at the depot—we'd been home only a day. We got some cash and grabbed Twenty-One an hour later. We've been in Ogden a couple hours." His glance took in MacDonald and the others. "Where do we fit into the picture this time, Tom?"

Moran laughed. "That's getting to the point in a hurry. I might as well put our cards on the table; the Denver and Pacific is in a jam, out in Idaho. A little town called Mustang Gap. County seat. Couple thousand people—and every man jack of 'em against us— Gene, spread the map out here on the table. Rip, you and Grumpy step up and I'll explain things." He checked himself and, looking up, added, "You boys have heard, I suppose, that we're building a new line to the Coast."

"Yeh, we read about it and wondered why," Grumpy told him. "You got a first-class road across northern Nevada. We couldn't figger why you needed a second line, a couple hundred miles to the north."

"A lot of people are wondering," Ambrose MacDonald remarked with a chuckle. He clipped the end off an expensive cigar with his gold clipper and rolled the panatela around on his lips but did not light it. He had not smoked in years but seldom was seen without a cigar in his mouth. "The Idaho line will open up a lot of new country."

"Plenty," Rainbow agreed. "Especially if you're pointing for the Pacific Northwest."

Little Ambrose tightened up instantly. "That's for the future to say," was his tart response.

Moran ignored the exchange. With the partners looking over his shoulder, he moved his pencil along the route of the present road across Nevada and stopped when he reached a dot on the map marked *Lander*.

Without looking up, he said, "You fellows know Lander. From Lander, a branch runs up across the Idaho line to Mustang Gap. There it is, there."

"And that's where it meets the new road?" Rainbow inquired.

"No—and that's the rub!" Moran slung his pencil on the table. "It was our intention to go through Mustang Gap. We had our engineers out there for weeks running surveys and figuring costs. This gap the town was named for is a deep, wide canyon. We couldn't find a way to get around it; to cross it would have cost a quarter of a million dollars. So we're by-passing the town—going through about fifteen miles north."

He went on to say that the D. and P. intended to extend the branch line to connect with the new road.

"Mustang Gap won't be left high and dry at the end of a stub line; it will have good service," Ambrose MacDonald hastened to add. "But that crowd out there isn't satisfied; they took it for granted that they'd be a main-line town—perhaps a division point—and cash in on it. But there's more to it than that; land values have climbed out of sight. Worthless wasteland has changed hands half a dozen times in the past six months. Range that was selling for thirty to forty dollars an acre—and no takers—has been whipped up to ten to twenty times what it's worth. Garner can tell you about that; he's been out there for weeks."

The D. and P.'s Chief of Detectives nodded phlegmatically. He had seen so much trouble in his long years of service that he rarely permitted himself to get excited. "They were all set to make us pay through the nose for a right of way. That's reason number two for what we've run into. They figure they got slapped down right and left. That's why men who wouldn't ordinarily stand for the deal we're getting are going along with it. I mean a man like Jarvis, the district court judge; the district attorney; Jim Lockhart, the sheriff. It's become common practice for McCandless's crew to run into gunfire from the hills when they go out to work in the morning. No one's been killed, but half a dozen got nipped. One night when Mac had Eyetalians working for him, a dozen or more mounted men raced through camp with their guns blazing and riddled the work train. That was enough for the Eyetalians."

"Hell," McCandless snorted, "how could you blame 'em for quitting? I got a couple hundred Chinks on the job now, and they're getting spooky. Cook tent pulled down a couple times—burned last week—more shooting—equipment wrecked—stakes pulled up! We've lost four or five weeks already. Be snowing before we get into Oregon, at this rate!"

"And you mean to tell us you can't find out who's spearheadin' all this trouble?" Grumpy demanded incredulously.

"Sure I know!" Garner replied hotly. "I've known for weeks. I swore out warrants against him three times. What happened? When he came up for arraignment, the cases were thrown out for lack of evidence."

"Who is he?" Rainbow asked.

"An outsider. He showed up in Mustang Gap about five months ago and began buying land and getting options on a lot of property. He's got an office in town and claims to be in the real estate and insurance business. He's just a big roughneck. Calls himself Ben Slade."

The partners' surprise was mutual.

"Wal, I'll be danged!" Grumpy exclaimed, slapping his knee. "What do you know about that, Rip?"

It brought Moran and the others to the edge of their chairs.

"Are we to understand that the two of you are acquainted with this man Slade?" Ambrose MacDonald snapped out.

Rainbow pulled down the corners of his mouth. "We've met up with him. The last time was in northern California. We were out there for the Grandby Logging and Lumber Company. Slade and a gang of timber pirates were destroying flumes and burning down sawmills. It was all part of a scheme to wreck the Grandby Company and grab a forty-thousand-acre tract of virgin pine. He tossed a stick of dynamite into a cabin where we were sleeping one night. We got out just in time."

"We'd have been pickin' somethin' bigger'n slivers outa our hides if we hadn't," Grumpy growled. "Slade and a couple others went to the pen before we got through with 'em. We never did git our hands on the gent who was bossin' that gang of crooks. But it wasn't Ben Slade; he's never been better than Number-Two man any time we've run up ag'in him."

"That's my hunch this trip," said Rainbow. "If he's been buying land, you can be sure it isn't his money he's using. But that's beside the point for the present." He turned to Moran. "Just what is it you want us to do, Tom?"

"I want you to go out there and get Slade dead to rights—bring him in with so much evidence against him that the authorities will have to act." Moran's tone was coldly sober. "Pat will go out with you. That will give him a chance to fill you in on all the details. You won't have a friend in that town. Slade will know why you're there. He'll turn his wolves loose on you. No use trying to pretend that it won't be a dangerous assignment. I won't talk price; you write your own ticket. What do you say?"

The partners exchanged a glance before giving him their answer. It was hardly necessary, for they had reached a decision the moment Ben Slade had appeared in the picture; their memories were long, and it wasn't only his attempt to blow them to kingdom come, that night in the cabin out in California, that needed squaring.

"When do we leave?" Rainbow asked, with a grin.

"Wait a minute, Grump, before you light that lamp," Rip exclaimed, his tone sharp and urgent, as they stepped into their room on the second floor of the Idaho House, in Mustang Gap, four days later. "Let's find out how tough this town is going to be for us."

They had ridden in from the railroad construction camp at the end of steel, northeast of town, just at sunset. After quartering their broncs in the hotel barn, they had taken a stroll up and down the main street before supper. Mustang Gap, with its brick bank and numerous saloons, was like a hundred other dusty cow towns they had seen in their time. A sign in the window enabled them to locate Ben Slade's real estate office without having to question anyone. Of Slade himself, they had failed to catch a glimpse.

"What's the idea?" the little one demanded as he saw Rainbow peel off his shirt and button it around a pillow from the bed and set it up in a chair.

"This fellow is too low; give me the other pillow," the tall man said, ignoring the question. "I'll need something to make him a neck. The towels will do. Roll them up."

"Good grief!" Grumpy exploded. "Why you makin' a dummy? This is jest hoss play!"

"Yeh?" Rip's tone was sober enough now. "When I top this thing off with my hat, and shove the chair over in front of the window, the lamplight ought to throw a reasonable facsimile of me on the shade. If we're being watched—and I reckon we are—don't be surprised if a slug comes crashing in here."

It took him only a minute or two to finish. Telling Grumpy to hold the lamp steady, he pushed the table on which it stood to the center of the room, so that the shadow would be sharp when it was cast on the window shade.

"You get over to the other window now, Grump, and peek out at the edge of the shade. If there's a shot, it'll come from the roof of one of the buildings across the street. Try to catch the gun flash. I'll light the lamp and drop down on the floor."

The seconds ticked away as he lay stretched out on the bedroom's worn carpet. Nothing happened.

"Had yore trouble for nuthin'," Grumpy muttered from the window. "Nobody over there."

"Don't be in a hurry," Rip flung back. "We'll stay put a few minutes."

Even as he finished speaking, a bullet shattered a pane of glass, cut through the crown of Rip's Stetson, and plowed into the room's rear wall.

"Did you catch the flash?" Rainbow whipped out.

"Yeh—over there on the roof of the lodge hall!"

The frame building, which housed a drugstore on the street floor, was dark. An outside stairway led up to the hall.

"Come on!" Rip barked, already at the door. "Let's get over there! I'll go up the stairs; you go around in back!"

CHAPTER TWO

THE SHOT ATTRACTED immediate attention. When the partners rushed into the hotel office, they found it crowded. They had almost reached the door when they came face to face with Gid Penny, the town marshal. He demanded an explanation, but they pushed him aside and raced across the street.

Rainbow found the door to the lodge room fastened with a snap lock. Using the barrel of his .45, he knocked out a small pane of glass above the lock, reached in, and opened the door.

In the reflected light from the street, the hall appeared to be deserted. He moved about cautiously, far from sure that he was alone. At the rear of the room, an old-fashioned roll-top desk had been moved out from the wall. A wooden box had been placed on top of it. Directly above the desk, a trap door stood open. Rip could see the stars shining through.

It dispelled any doubt as to how the gunman had reached the roof. As Rip stood there, listening, a shot sounded in the alley in back of the building. The tall man thought he recognized the familiar bark of Grumpy's long-barreled Frontier Model Colt.

For a brief minute the night was still again, and then someone ran up the back steps to the second-story porch, raised a ladder that lay there, and reached the roof.

Rainbow could hear him moving around. Footsteps approached the open trap door then. Rip crouched behind the desk. A moment later the man on the roof peered cautiously down into the lodge room.

"Grump!" Rip cried, recognizing the little figure silhouetted against the sky. "What was that shot?"

"I was jest in time to see a fella dartin' down the alley. I called on him to throw up his hands. When he didn't stop, I snapped a shot at him. But he was gone. Hold that box steady and I'll come down."

Though he was in his late fifties, he was as agile as most men half his age. With some grunting, he lowered himself and found the box with his feet. He froze there, his eyes narrowing in his hard-bitten face as he caught the sullen babbling of the crowd that was bearing down on the lodge hall. It was only a moment before they were pouring up the outside stairs.

"They're comin' for us, Rip! This may be trouble!"

The tall man nodded coolly. "Get down here beside me. This will be the marshal and his friends. Let me do the talking!"

The door was flung open, and Penny burst in, closely followed by a dozen men, their faces dark with anger.

"Stand where yuh are till I git some light in here!" the marshal ground out fiercely, backing up his command with drawn gun.

A lodge member lit a wall lamp. It flickered fitfully and threatened to go out until someone closed the door. In the uncertain yellow light Gid Penny's round face seemed to be all jowls. He was a squat little man, with a drooping mustache.

"Now what was the idear, bustin' the door and breakin' into this hall?" he began again, simmering with wrath.

Rainbow told him what had occurred and tried to tell him who he and Grumpy were. He didn't get far with that.

"I know who yuh are!" Penny growled. "You're a couple Denver and Pacific spies!"

"Is that what Ben Slade told you?" the tall man asked calmly.

It threw the marshal into a greater frenzy. The dozen or more men who had rushed in with him drew themselves up threateningly. "Keep Slade's name out of this!"

"Why are you so anxious to keep his name out of it?" Rainbow demanded with the same maddening absence of excitement that had infuriated Penny and the others. "If you knew his record, maybe you wouldn't be—"

"I know all about his record! He got in some trouble in Californy fightin' them timber barons. He squared that.

Yuh won't git nowheres around here with that kind of talk!"

A wiry individual, with a cadaverous face and a scrawny neck, opened the door and pushed up to the marshal. He had a silver star pinned on his vest. It told the partners that this was Sheriff Jim Lockhart.

"Gid, I know you're responsible for the peace of this town, but if you don't mind, I'll take over."

The sheriff squared around on the partners, his eyes burning with hostility and ordered them to put their guns back in the leather.

"I want you fellas to git this straight right now," he continued. "Don't try to take the law into yore own hands in this county. Jest because yo're a couple private detectives don't give you any special rights or privileges."

Rainbow knew what Grumpy and he were up against, but his lean face betrayed no sign of emotion. "Sheriff," he said in his quiet way, "somebody thought he was putting a slug into me. Do you call it a special privilege for a man to try to find out who was throwing lead at him?"

"No lead was thrown at you, Ripley. I had a look at your room before I came up here. Shovin' a dummy up in front of the window was purty crude stuff. If you wanted the shot investigated, the marshal was around, and so was I."

"It isn't too late for you to do something about it—if you're inclined that way," Rip observed, his smile as contemptuous as his tone. "Not that you'd get far. I don't believe Slade would let you."

There was no mistaking his meaning. He saw the Mustang Gap men present regarding the sheriff with an obscure interest as they waited for his answer, and he surmised correctly that this was not the first time that Lockhart's relations with Ben Slade had been questioned.

The sheriff flicked a glance at them and promptly decided that he might better ignore the accusation and hurry on to something else. He mentioned the shot in the alley.

"You didn't know who you was shootin' at," he rapped. "That man was goin' about his lawful business. He happened to be Chet Yaples, the postmaster—as harmless a man as ever lived. I'm tellin' the two of you right now, that kinda highhanded stuff don't go with me. You pull anythin' like that a second time and I'm lockin' you up. If you'll take my advice, you'll clear out of the Gap and stay out!"

"No, Sheriff," Rip said firmly, "we're sticking around till we're convinced that the difference between this town and the Denver and Pacific can't be settled peacefully and in a manner satisfactory to both sides."

"Not a chance!" Penny ripped out, with a jeering grunt. "Yo're wastin' yore time!"

"I'll say you are!" Lockhart agreed with equal vehemence. "Nobody will lissen to you!"

"I think they will when they begin to realize that this is a three-cornered fight and that they're being caught in the middle of it." Rainbow was speaking to the men now, not to the sheriff and the marshal. "I know it's becoming pretty obvious to some of you that certain parties must be making a good thing out of it or they wouldn't be whooping up this fight with the railroad. When this trouble started, weeks ago, it would have been an easy matter for the company to have brought in a couple hundred gunmen and turned them loose on you. That wasn't done, and we've been guaranteed that nothing of the sort will be done; we know it's just a matter of time when you folks will wake up to the fact that you're just being used to pull Slade's coals out of the fire. When that happens, an agreement can be reached in a hurry."

Lockhart and Penny scoffed as expected and pretended to find it all very amusing. It didn't fool Rainbow. Watching the faces of the men, he saw two or three wavering in their loyalty to the sheriff and the marshal. He caught Grumpy's eye, and the two of them started for the door. The Mustang Gap men drew aside to let them pass. Lockhart was about to stop them, when he pulled back and let them go without a word.

"Never kept my mouth shut so long in my life!" the little one sputtered as they went down the stairs. "If that gent I caught duckin' down the alley really was the postmaster, he may have been on his lawful business, but it was none of Uncle Sam's business, I can tell you. If I had wanted to knock him over, I'd a done it. The slug was five feet over his head. I figgered it might scare him enough to stop him. I don't go around bangin' away at people 'less I know who they are. Why didn't you tell that badge-totin' stringbean so?"

"Don't whip yourself up into a tizzy over nothing," Rainbow advised. "I didn't say anything because I had bigger fish to fry. You won't hear anything further about it from the sheriff. Slade owns him and the marshal lock, stock, and barrel. It's my guess that he's got to the district attorney and the judge as well. Lockhart knew what I was driving at. He had the opportunity to sound off, but he didn't want any part of it."

"You bet he didn't—not when he saw how eager some of the crowd was to hear what he had to say for himself. These Mustang Gap folks ain't so dumb; they don't know what the setup is yet, but they're gittin' suspicious."

"I hope you're right," was the tall man's tight-lipped response.

"No hopin' about it; you know I'm right!" Grumpy insisted. "Do you think Lockhart would have let you git away with all that gab if he wasn't out on thin ice? Separatin' the sheep from the goats ain't goin' to be as tough a job as we figgered."

They reached the plank sidewalk and cut across the street, their boots kicking up little spurts of dust. The night was still young, and groups of men gathered in front of the saloons turned their heads and gave the partners a careful, hostile scrutiny. The latter pretended not to be aware of the attention leveled at them.

Up the street, a whisky-brave cowboy in faded overalls and frayed Stetson flung himself into the saddle and dashed at them, apparently intent on running them down.

"Steady," Rip muttered. "This fellow is only showing off."

The plunging bronc bore down on them swiftly, but

they refused to hurry their step. Being well acquainted with the character of cow ponies, they knew the average animal would avoid them if given half a chance. This one proved to be no exception to the rule and veered off at the last split second, only the off stirrup brushing across Grumpy's back as it flashed by.

It was an exhibition of cool nerve that was calculated to make a deeper impression on Mustang Gap than mere gunplay. Of the spectators, no one had been more interested than the burly, heavy-featured man who sat on the porch of the Idaho House. He flung his frayed cigar away with an angry curse as he saw Rip and Grumpy coming up the steps unscathed.

"Ben Slade," Rainbow said, recognizing him instantly and rubbing the surprise out of his voice. "Did you arrange that little trick?"

"No," Slade replied, "I hadn't thought of it. I wish I had."

Physically, he had changed very little since the partners had seen him last, but his clothes were better and his self-assurance more pronounced.

"I heard you showed up out at the camp a couple days ago," he volunteered, and added with an insolent grin, "I knew I'd be seein' you. Did you figger I was goin' to run?"

"Not right away," Rip said lightly. "You've been spreading some money around, Ben. Who are you fronting for this time?"

Slade's rasping laugh was loud but held very little amusement. "It'd surprise you, wouldn't it, if I was usin' my own money?"

"Surprise wouldn't begin to be the word for it," the tall man told him. "You didn't have a buck to your name when you were sent up; and you haven't been out more than three or four months."

"Mebbe I had some dough stashed away," was the big man's insolent rejoinder. His counterfeit amiability was gone, and his narrowed eyes were hard and frosty with the hatred he bore the partners. "Where I get my money and how I spend it is none of your damn business! You guys go ahead with your snoopin'. If you get in my way, I'll know what to do about it. You'll find out before you get very far that I got this town solid in back of me."

It wrung a scornful grunt out of Grumpy. "Yo're countin' chickens that ain't hatched yet, Slade. But that's a habit with you. Why don't you git wise to yoreself? The Denver and Pacific ain't goin' to buy none of yore land. That issue was decided weeks ago; the road will go through up north as planned and all the hell you been raisin' makes that dead certain."

"So I'm just bangin' my head against a stone wall for nothin', eh?" Slade hauled himself to his feet and expressed his boredom with a loud yawn. "Railroad companies change their plans, same as anyone else, when they find the goin' gettin' too expensive."

A man came up the steps and said, "Ben, can I see you for a minute?"

Slade said, "Sure, Nate," and walked into the bar with him. The partners went on upstairs.

"He figgers he's holdin' a handful of aces this time," the little one grunted.

"Maybe he is," Rip said, with a shrug. "That leaves the joker running wild. I reckon we'll take a trick or two."

CHAPTER THREE

THE PARTNERS walked into the office of the Mustang Gap *Item* in the morning and introduced themselves to Mark Wigg, the editor-owner of the newspaper.

"We are out here on behalf of the Denver and Pacific Railroad," Rip told him.

"So I understand," Wigg said. "I heard what happened last evening. I know you by reputation, of course. All the Nevada papers are on my exchange list, so I am familiar with some of the things you've accomplished." He was an angular, sharp-featured man with a pair of shrewd, intelligent eyes behind his steel-rimmed spectacles. "What can I do for you, gentlemen?"

"I got hold of some back copies of the *Item* last night," Rainbow informed him. "The tone of your hard-hitting editorials surprised us. In view of the trouble the company has had for the past month, we hardly expected to find the local newspaper condemning what had been going on as wanton outlawry."

Wigg's eyes twinkled. "You'll hardly be surprised to know that, next to yourselves, I am the most unpopular man in Mustang Gap because of the stand I've taken. I've been threatened, and Slade has tried to bribe me; but I don't scare easily, and I'm not for sale."

"That's more than some others could say, I reckon," Grumpy observed pointedly. "And I ain't referrin' to private citizens."

The owner of the *Item* nodded grimly. "I know who you mean. I can't prove it, but there's no doubt in my mind but what they've been bribed. Have you been up to the courthouse?"

"Not yet," said Rip.

"Well, you'll get a cool reception from Judge Jarvis and Bemis Price, the prosecutor. You know, of course, that Slade has been charged with destruction of railroad property on several occasions. Price has always moved for dismissal for lack of evidence. Jarvis has gone along with him. I don't pretend to be a lawyer, but there was evidence enough to warrant holding Slade for trial. That wasn't done, and knowing the facts, it didn't surprise me."

"What do you mean—knowin' the facts?" Grumpy asked bluntly.

"Why, when we first heard that the railroad was coming through, Henry Jarvis bought a lot of land on the other side of the gap. In my mind that disqualifies him to sit on any matter concerning the Denver and Pacific. He's certainly interested to the tune of a few thousand dollars in having the road come across the gap instead of cutting through to the north."

This was news to the partners and they did not attempt to minimize the importance they attached to it. Wigg said further that it was generally known that Jarvis had a personal stake in the fight.

"But the town goes along with him because everyone figures he's got a stake in this scrap, too," Rainbow suggested.

"That's right," the editor agreed. "They figure they got a raw deal, so they stand for a lot; but they're not being fooled, and only a handful have actually taken part in all this violence and destruction of railroad property. This town is no different than any other; we have some riffraff. Slade had no trouble lining them up. He uses them, but the men he depends on are the five or six thugs he brought in with him."

The partners had already learned as much for themselves.

"You mean Pete Cleary, Nate Flood, and that bunch?" Grumpy muttered. "Ike Miggles is another. They're known gunmen. We was tipped off to be on the lookout for 'em before we got out here. Only five or six of 'em, eh?"

"Just five or six. You'll see them hanging around Slade's office or in the hotel barroom. They're pretty cocky. They wouldn't be if you could turn the town against them. That could be done easily enough."

"I don't know what you have in mind," Rainbow remarked, more interested than he let on, "but if you have an idea, we'd certainly be glad to hear it." He was rapidly becoming convinced that they had discovered an unexpected ace in the hole in the shrewd, hardheaded editor of the *Item*.

"It's simply this," the latter declared without hesitation; "let the Denver and Pacific give Mustang Gap some visible proof that it means what it says about building the branch line up to connect with the transcontinental line. So far, all we've had is a promise that binds the company to nothing."

"The connecting link will be built," Rip protested. "The advantage in hooking up the Idaho road with the Nevada system must be apparent to you."

Wigg nodded. "It is. But that's not the general attitude around here. It would be a simple matter to bring material up from Lander and start laying track. Our merchants would get some business out of it and the feeling against the company would change over night. Inside of a week Ben Slade would be on his own. Even the judge and Jim Lockhart would walk out on him. No one runs for shore any quicker than a politician when he sees the tide going against him."

"Mister, that makes sense to me!" Grumpy slapped his hat on the counter to better express his convictions. "Yo're a hundred-percent right!" He gave Rainbow a scowling glance. "You see anythin' wrong with it?"

"Not a thing," the tall man answered thoughtfully. "The dirt would be flying in a few days if I were making company policy. But I certainly shall ask Moran and Ambrose MacDonald to meet us in Lander next week so we can discuss the idea with them."

He thanked Wigg for the help he had been, and before leaving, he arranged to have a reward notice published in the *Item*. A few minutes later, Grumpy and he found themselves on the street. Instead of going to the courthouse, as they had intended, they turned back to the hotel. Halfway to the corner, they ran into Lockhart. The sheriff had been standing there waiting for them for some time.

"I see you been in talkin' to Mark Wigg," he said, his tone curt and hostile. "Yo're kiddin' yoreselves if you think he cuts any ice around here. He's lucky he ain't been run outa town, considerin' what he's been printin'. You shore didn't lose any time lookin' him up!"

It gave Rainbow the opening he wanted. "We had a little business for the *Item*. The company is offering twenty-five hundred dollars for information leading to the arrest and conviction of the parties responsible for the destruction of company property and interfering with the construction of the new road."

"You won't git nowheres with that!" Lockhart grunted contemptuously. Under Rip's steady gaze, he was uncomfortable, however, and he could not conceal it.

"We'll see," said the tall man. "They say that money talks. Some men will do a lot for twenty-five hundred dollars. If that doesn't do the trick, we'll raise the ante. The D. and P. has more money to spend than Ben Slade. Or maybe you mean that we won't get a conviction no matter what the evidence is. If that's your idea, you better forget it; company lawyers are in Boise right now discussing the situation down here with the attorney general. He has the authority to supersede or remove from office any district judge or other county official who is derelict in his duty."

It shook Lockhart. "Whoa right there!" he bellowed, the folds of his thin, leathery face filling out with rage. "You tryin' to say that me and the judge ain't been doin' our duty?"

"No, I was just pointing out some unpleasant possibilities," Rip informed him coolly. "If the shoe doesn't fit, there's no reason why you should put it on. We'll see you later, Sheriff."

Lockhart was glad to see them go.

Once they were out of earshot, Grumpy began to sputter. "What's eating you?" Rip asked.

"That wild talk about the attorney general! The company's got nobody up in Boise!"

The tall man grinned. "Pure, unadulterated bluff," he

acknowledged. "But Lockhart and Jarvis won't call it. I reckon if you had eyes in the back of your head you'd see Lockhart hotfooting it up to the courthouse right now. It'll give that pair something to think about."

"I'm danged if you don't sound as though you was enjoyin' yoreself!" the little one grumbled.

"I am, for a fact," said Rip. "We'll try to give their tails another twist or two as we go along."

From the information they had gathered at the construction camp, supplemented by what Pat Garner had been able to tell them, the partners knew more about the men with whom Slade had surrounded himself than they had given the editor of the *Item* reason to believe. The type was a familiar one—hard-faced, ignorant men, as much at home in jail as out of it, and who, for wages, were always ready to engage in any lawless enterprise. However, Rip and Grumpy were anxious to come face to face with Flood, Cleary, Ike Miggles, and the others and size them up at first hand.

Crossing the street, they glanced up at Slade's office as they passed. There was no sign of anyone up there. They tried the Idaho House bar only to find it deserted, save for a couple of dusty-looking stockmen and the bartender. Making the rounds of the other saloons proved equally unprofitable. Returning to the hotel, they sat down on the porch. It was an excellent vantage point from which to observe the life of the town and keep an eye on Slade's office. The better part of an hour passed before they were convinced that they were wasting their time.

"What do you make of it?" Rainbow queried.

The little one shook his head. "I dunno," he muttered, frankly perplexed. "I figgered Slade would make a point of gittin' in our way jest to let us see how big a man he is around here, if for no other reason."

"Exactly," said Rip. "You sit here a few minutes longer; I'm going up to his office and try the door."

He wasn't gone long. "No one there," he reported. "The door was unlocked. I walked in and had a look around. Let's go back to the barn and see if one of the stablemen can tell us where that bunch keep their broncs."

They found Dobe Roberts, the barn boss, seated in the doorway, dozing in the sun. As a rule, he had little to do after the early-morning hours until evening rolled around again. His head came up as he saw the partners crossing the yard to the barn.

"Wal," he cackled good-naturedly, "you boys still seem to be in one piece." Screwing up his old eyes, he gave the bullet hole in Rip's Stetson a piercing squint. "Reckon you'd have got yore last haircut if yore head had been in the hat when that slug slapped into it. You want yore hosses?"

"No." Grumpy spoke up. "We're tryin' to locate Slade and his boys. Where do they keep their broncs?"

"Right hyar," the old man answered, on guard instantly.

"Do you mind if we have a look at them?" said Rainbow.

"Don't know as there'd be any harm in that," Dobe answered, wiping his mouth with the back of his hand and weighing his words carefully. "If the hosses was in the barn. But they ain't." His eyes roamed the yard, making sure they were alone. Lowering his voice, he added, "Slade and his gang pulled out fer the north jest after daylight. Gave me hell becuz I didn't jump fast enough to suit 'em." He snapped his jaws together resentfully. "I'm jest a banged-up old buckaroo, but I'm damned if I got any use for them blacklegs, railroad or no railroad!"

Rainbow moved closer and squatted down on his heels. "Dobe—you know where they were heading?"

"I ain't supposed to know. If I say anythin' and it gits back to 'em, they'll bust me loose from my job."

Rip pressed a five-dollar gold piece into the old man's hand. "Anything you say to us won't get any further. Where they going?"

"Mud Springs. That's where they camp."

"You know how to get there?"

"Shore! I used to go to the Springs to shoot sage hen, years ago. Take the road north and stay with it till you see some rounded hills off to the west. Swing that way about three mile."

"Will we find a trail that'll take us into the Springs?"

"There's an old trail. But you could miss it. Better not try to locate it till yo're a mile or so off the road. Start lookin' for a clump of aspens. You'll see 'em down in a little coulee. Go down to the trees and scout around; you'll pick up the trail. It crawls over some low ridges. From the third one, you'll see some more aspens and a patch of green down below. That'll be Mud Springs."

Simple as the directions were, Rainbow repeated them, making doubly sure that he understood them correctly. "How many men did Slade have with him this morning, Dobe?"

"Five—Flood, Cleary, Fanin, Santell, and Ike Miggles. They showed up with a couple pack animals. The packs was heavy."

"Do they usually pack in like that?" Grumpy demanded suspiciously. "It couldn't be grub—not that much."

"Reckon not," the old man agreed. "If it was grub, they'd a tied it on their saddles." He took off his battered hat and scratched his head thoughtfully. "I don't know what was in the packs, but they was tied mighty careful."

"You know hosses." Grumpy continued to prod. "Where did they git the animals?"

"Rented 'em from Ab Jenkins. He does most of the packin' and freightin' out of the Gap. But that won't tell you what you want to know. If there was anythin' in them packs that Slade didn't want folks to see, the packin' wa'n't done in Ab's barn. Most likely it was done down on the crick. Cleary and Miggles led the hosses in here. They had wet mud on their boots."

"It doesn't matter," said Rip. "You get our broncs saddled, Dobe. We're going to Mud Springs. We'll be back as soon as we settle our hotel bill."

Grumpy had to hurry to catch up with him as he led the way back to the street. "You swallowin' everythin' that old juniper had to say for gospel?" the little man growled.

"Why not?" Rip snapped. "We got the information we wanted."

"And it could be walkin' us into a massacre! Ben Slade wouldn't want nothin' better than to git us out in the hills and knock us off. This whole deal could be a frame-up, and you know it!"

"No—not a chance in a thousand," Rainbow said firmly. "Slade had no reason to think for a minute that we'd be talking to the barn boss. We'll keep our eyes open; but I aim to see Mud Springs and find out what was in those packs."

Rainbow kept looking back over his shoulder as he and Grumpy jogged along. Mustang Gap was rapidly dropping behind. Ahead of them the road uncoiled for miles across unfenced sagebrush flats. There was no water here, and no cattle; the cattle were up on the benchlands, far to the east, where Shoshone Creek broke through the mountains.

"We bein' followed?" the little one asked as Rip scanned their back trail again. The latter shook his head. Mustang Gap had dropped from sight and they had the road to themselves.

Half an hour later they passed a deserted sheep camp. The rock corral was still intact, but the sun-warped cabin was falling apart. A mile beyond the cabin, Grumpy pulled his bronc down to a walk.

"Here's where we turned into the road yesterday afternoon, Rip. I marked the spot by that cut-bank. That's Split Rock Mountain rearin' up over there to the northeast."

Rainbow said, "We can't get lost around here with a landmark like that to show us the way home."

The railroad construction camp was now located not more than a mile east of Split Rock Mountain. Glacial action, or some other violent movement of the earth's crust, had sheared off the southern slope of Split Rock, leaving a rocky face that rose almost perpendicularly from the plains to the crumbling rim. In order to avoid the mountain's sliced-off shoulder, the Denver and Pacific engineers were sending the tracks through the opening in and within a few yards of Split Rock's bald face.

A moving cloud of dust topped a swell in the road ahead of the partners and brought them to attention just when the rounded hills off to the west that old Dobe had told them to look for were beginning to loom up on the horizon. The dust cloud resolved itself into a team of ratty-looking mustangs drawing a buckboard. An elderly couple, a rancher and his wife by their appearance, were seated in the rig. Rip hailed them, and the man pulled up.

"Did you pass a bunch of men this morning—six in the party—and a couple pack horses?"

"We didn't pass no one, but we saw some riders cuttin' across the flats," the driver of the buckboard answered. "There was five or six of 'em, I'd say."

"Was they headin' for Mud Springs?" asked Grumpy.

"No, they was too far north—and headin' the opposite way. Some of them railroad fellers, I reckon."

"I allow as how they was," the little one declared. "Much obliged to you, stranger." He raised his hand to hat in a parting salute, and the couple drove on.

Rainbow said, "That wasn't any party of engineers he saw; that was Slade's bunch."

"Of course it was!" the little one snapped. "I was jest agreein' with that old-timer to git rid of him. McCandless ain't got nobody roamin' around this far west of the mountain. When he gits by Split Rock, he'll have that wide dry wash starin' him in the eye. He told me the other day that he wasn't goin' to attempt to do anythin' over here till he'd thrown a trestle across the wash and moved camp again." He wagged his head soberly. "I don't know how you feel about it, but I got a hunch that Slade is dishin' up somethin' extra special for us." His hard-bitten face was as grim as his tone. "We better try to pick up his trail and forgit about Mud Springs. We won't find nobody there."

"It isn't likely we will," Rip acknowledged. "But that's all the more reason for having a look at their camp; we may find something that will give us a clue to what he's got on his mind."

The doughty little man saw some wisdom in the suggestion, but he, as was his habit, gave in grudgingly.

At quickened pace, the partners moved along for another mile and then cut westward across the sage. They had no difficulty finding the coulee with the clump of aspens that Dobe Roberts had mentioned. There they picked up the trail into the Springs. Fresh horse droppings were proof enough that it had been used in the last few hours.

Forty minutes later they crested a low ridge and saw Slade's camp down below. A tarp had been stretched between trees. Beneath it, protected from the sun, were blankets and odds and ends of camp equipment. Smoke still spiraled lazily skyward from a fire.

Rainbow studied the camp with a pair of binoculars for several minutes. "Don't see anyone down there," he said, handing the glasses to Grumpy. "Take a look."

The little man examined every square yard of the camp. "No one there," he muttered. "Reckon we can go down."

The provisions and camp gear stored under the tarpaulin told them nothing. The discovery of a heavy canvas sack, filled with rifle and revolver cartridges, was no more than they had expected to find. Outside, at the fire, however, a number of small wooden boxes had been opened and broken up for kindling. Grumpy pounced on a piece and his eyes widened as he read the word stenciled on the board.

"Rip, look at this! *Dynamite!* And here's another—and another! That's what was in the packs!"

Rainbow refused to get excited. "That was my hunch from the beginning."

"But they brought in enough to blow down a mountain!"

The tall man's smile was hard and bright and devoid of mirth. "Maybe that's the idea."

"Split Rock, you mean?"

"Yeh! Thank God we found out now! McCandless plans to have his pick-and-shovel men working in close to the base of Split Rock tomorrow! Come on! We're getting back to camp!"

CHAPTER FOUR

NOON WAS LONG GONE by the time the partners climbed out of the dry wash two miles west of Split Rock Mountain. Swinging wide, so that they could scrutinize the mountain carefully with the glasses, they spent a quarter of an hour trying to find some sign of activity along its southern face. If there was anyone up there, Rainbow and the little one failed to locate them.

At camp, the daily work train, with the antiquated day coach that the construction personnel used in traveling back and forth from the east, had arrived. Chinese laborers were unloading ties and rails. All told, McCandless had a force of two hundred Orientals. Under Chinese bosses, a good half of them were throwing up roadbed; a short distance away, others were slicing off a hillside with pick and shovel and slip scrapers.

"Reckon them mules never heard no jabberin' like that before," Grumpy observed as he saw a Chinese skillfully maneuvering his team.

Rip smiled. "I doubt it, Grump. But the work gets done—or it would if those yellow boys were given half a chance. We'll ride over to the headquarters car and see Mac at once."

The office on wheels stood on a temporary siding, along with the car in which McCandless lived. Coupled to them were the old Pullmans that his engineers and assistants occupied. The big cook tent was situated on the other side of camp, and behind it, on another siding, the long line of made-over boxcars which housed the crew.

McCandless was not at his desk when the partners stepped into the office. Before they could ask the clerk as to his whereabouts, he hurried across the platform of his own car and joined them. They had found the D. and P.'s Chief of Construction a gruff, taciturn man, whose sense of humor had disappeared completely in the face of the difficulties that were bogging down the building of the new road. His tone was unexpectedly cordial, however, as he asked the partners to sit down.

"I don't know who should talk first—me or you," he continued. "I have a surprise for the two of you—especially for you, Ripley. I guess it'll keep for a minute. How did you make out in town?"

Rainbow recounted what had happened in Mustang Gap the previous evening and that morning. Mark Wigg's suggestion was received enthusiastically by McCandless.

"That's a damned good idea, starting work on the branch line at once!" he exclaimed. "We've got a wire here. Ambrose MacDonald is our man. We'll get a message off to him right away. You can meet him in Lander, or I will. From what you have to say, things ain't as bad as I thought. If you can get Slade out on the end of a limb—"

"They're bad enough," Grumpy interjected. "This situation ain't goin' to be licked in a day or two. Slade's got somethin' cookin' right now that'll need some stoppin'. Tell him what we found at Mud Springs, Rip."

What Rainbow had to say pulled McCandless out of his chair. "It's Split Rock Mountain they're after, sure enough! Thank God you got wind of it in time. If my Chinamen got caught in the cut when that wall came crashing down, it would be like killing sheep! Ripley, you and your partner have got to stop that gang!"

"You'll have to give us a little time," said Rainbow. "Don't allow any of your men to work in close to the mountain for a few days."

"You can count on that," McCandless assured him. "All that's needed right now is to have a couple of these Chinks killed and the whole crew will walk off the job." He mopped his perspiring face for a moment. "I know they been getting restless, but I'm damned if I had any idea that they were ready to ask for their time till an hour or so ago. These Chinks don't tell you what they're thinking. They ain't like a gang of Italians. They got their *padrone* or head man. They do their talking to him."

"That would be Quan Jee," said Rip.

"Yeh, the big man with the knife scar across his chin They'd be back in California by now if it wasn't for him. Quan's been holding them on the job till he could get someone up from San Francisco who could talk to 'em. She got here on today's train. She thinks she can persuade the men to stay. She may change her mind when she hears what Slade is up to now."

Rainbow and Grumpy sat up in tight-lipped surprise; they knew of only one Chinese woman who wielded that sort of influence over her people.

"She—you say?" the tall man said, trying to master his surprise.

"Yeh— A Miss Seng. Quan calls her Seng Mei-lang, but I understand that's just the Chinese way of twisting names." The ghost of a smile touched McCandless's tanned face. "That was the little surprise I said I had for you. And a beautiful suprise she is. I never realized how damned shabby my car was till she stepped into it. I understand the three of you are well acquainted."

"By grab, that ain't the half of it!" Grumpy declared heartily. "Miss Seng has been our good angel for years. Wimmen don't come any finer than Mei-lang Seng. If she's here, you got nothin' to worry about, Mac!"

"I'll have to agree with that," Rainbow said quietly, his eyes focused on the carved jade ring he wore on his finger. Mei-lang had given it to him as a talisman four years back. Chinese referred to it as the ring of the Family of Seng. It had opened many doors and unsealed many lips for the tall man. "If Miss Seng advises your crew to stick, they'll stick. Where is she now?"

"In my car, waiting for you," McCandless answered. "Would you like to go in alone?"

The tall man nodded. "I'd appreciate it."

He hurried out, and Grumpy sat there, smiling to himself. He knew, as well as he knew anything, that Rainbow had been in love with Mei-lang for years and that it was only the absurd racial barrier that kept them apart. There were times when the little man doubted that that would always hold true. He didn't want to lose Rainbow to any woman, but if it ever had to be, he hoped it would be to Mei-lang.

Some wise man once said that a priceless jewel never loses its scintillating beauty no matter what its setting. It was true of Mei-lang. She didn't belong in this railroad construction camp or in this battered car, with its worn furnishings and masculine disorder. But Rainbow had found her before in drab surroundings and they had failed to detract from her fresh young loveliness. It was so this afternoon. She wore the traditional black of the high-caste Chinese woman, her sleek gown of brocaded silk, with its military collar and slitted skirt flattering even to her alluring figure.

She was standing at the window, gazing abstractedly at the gray desert landscape, when he opened the door. She turned to him eagerly, her dark eyes warm and bright with respect and affection.

Rainbow was at her side instantly and would have taken her in his arms had she not held him off, saying softly, "Not yet—please! I want to look at you! You seem taller and thinner. How long has it been since last we met?"

"Ten long months. Haven't you counted them?"

"Yes," she murmured. "They've been long months for me, too, my darling!"

To have her so near and yet so far away was too much for Rip. Unable to restrain himself further, he drew her close and found her red, yielding lips.

"Rainbow," she whispered, deep in his embrace, "if this moment had any meaning—any promise of a day to come for us, I couldn't stand it; I'd be too happy. But it's only a wonderful, precious dream that begins and ends in almost the same breath. It must always be so."

"I refuse to believe that," said Rip, his voice rough with feeling. "If we have the courage to break some of these chains and live our lives as we want to live them—"

"No," Mei-lang insisted regretfully, "the world wouldn't leave us alone. Its intolerance and prejudices would crucify our love. There'd be no happiness for us that way."

She looked up at him and smiled tenderly. "Don't be so distraught, my darling. We've been over all this so many times that both of us should know by now that there's no way out for us. I might remind you," she continued in a lighter tone, "that there are no curtains on the windows of this car."

"Mei-lang—is there someone else?"

"No! There'll never be anyone else for me. I have my work for the China Society to keep me busy—there is so much to be done for our people, and so few of us to do it."

Rainbow let her go. "Did you know I was here?"

"Not until Mr. McCandless told me. And Grumpy? How is he?"

"Crustier than ever and not getting any younger. McCandless just told us why you made the long trip up from California."

"It's very fortunate that I can talk things over with you. Shall we sit down? Naturally, I wouldn't like to see our men quit. We are proud of the reputation our Chinese laborers have earned of seeing through whatever they undertake. On the other hand, I could hardly ask them to remain if it means that they are to be shot at, killed, wounded, the camp raided at will. What are the conditions, Rainbow?"

"They've been bad, and they're likely to get worse for a few days. I don't believe we'll be raided again. The man who's behind all this trouble has had some previous acquaintance with Grump and me; he knows if he molests the camp again he'll run into gunfire. We have a number of white men here—timekeepers, clerks, surveyors. They're not fighting men. We'd be a lot safer if Quan Jee picked out two or three of his young men and turned them over to me to help stand guard. I haven't forgotten how those Chinese boys came through during that Wolf River trouble down in Nevada a year ago."

"I've already spoken to Quan Jee about you," said Mei-lang. "He'll do whatever you say. But you said things may get worse. How do you mean?"

He told her what he feared was about to happen.

"Maybe it won't come off; maybe we can prevent it. In any event, the crew should be told what to expect. If they know, there won't be any panic, and no one will get hurt. McCandless has given me his word, and I'll add mine to it, that no work will be done close in to the mountain until we know it's safe for the men to be there. Once the road gets beyond Split Rock, there's a wide dry wash. A trestle will have to be built. There may be some trouble there, but by that time I figure we'll have Slade on the run. You can see that you've come at a good time, Mei-lang."

She gazed at him soberly and with the unassailable dignity that was her great charm. "You sound confident, Rainbow. You don't mention your own danger. I know it will be great; but you always ignore the risks you run. I wish I could remain here and see this through with you."

To hear her speak of leaving tightened Rip's mouth. "When will you be going?"

"In the morning. Mr. McCandless has agreed to take me into Mustang Gap. I'll go back to California by way of Lander. It will save me about eight hundred miles. Perhaps we better ask Mr. McCandless to come in now. He can send for Quan Jee. I want to see Grumpy, too."

Rainbow got up. "I'll call them." At the door, he turned back. "I don't want to sway you, Mei-lang, but if you can persuade the men to stay on the job, they'll have at least a year's work ahead of them at good wages. I know you'll take that into consideration."

She smiled at him fondly. "How little you know me, Rainbow! My decision was made the moment I learned that you were here. We'll call the men together this evening. I know I can promise you that they won't be quitting."

Rainbow and Mei-lang strolled out from camp that evening. The desert stars were out in all their magnificent glory. To the east, a pale young moon hung low in the sky.

The meeting with Quan Jee and the big crew had resulted in a satisfactory accord. Rip had spoken briefly and heard himself cheered when Mei-lang translated his request for four men to act as armed guards. And yet he was silent and constrained in her company now. She was equally uncommunicative and answered with a little nod when he suggested that they had better turn back.

"This is good-by again." She sighed, as they stood there, with the night around them. "Who knows how long it will be before we meet again?"

"You could come to Wyoming this fall—if you can get away for a couple weeks. The 7 Bar is a comfortable place. We could hunt and fish. I know how well you ride. We could pack into the Wind River Mountains for a day or two. It's beautiful country. Would that appeal to you, Mei-lang?"

"It would be heaven!" She threw her arms about his neck impulsively. "Just to be with you anywhere would be heaven! I know Wyoming in the autumn must be wonderful."

"It's a date, then!" said Rainbow. "I'll be in touch with you and meet you in Black Forks."

They had reached the edge of camp—the evening was still young—when a terrific blast shook the earth. High above Split Rock Mountain, a cloud of dust mushroomed up into the sky, followed by the booming thunder of tons of rock hurtling down into the cut at the base of the mountain.

Save for the cooks and kitchen help, the Chinese crew had already sought their bunks for the night. They poured out of the cars now, wildly excited. But they had been warned to expect an explosion and there was no sign of panic among them. On the other siding, McCandless and his staff had flung aside their games and their reading and rushed outside, as excited and voluble as the crew.

Following the blast, the crunching, splintering rockfall sent wave after wave of angry rumbling rolling across the sagebrush plains.

"Rainbow—you didn't expect the blast to come tonight?" Mei-lang cried.

"No," he answered, "but I'm glad it did!" Catching her arm, he hurried her along until they found Quan Jee. The latter, a big, sinewy man with the strength of an elephant, could speak some English. Rip grinned at him.

"Those fellows lost their nerve, Quan!" he declared with what sounded like genuine satisfaction. "They were afraid my partner and I would be up on the mountain tomorrow. The joke's on them; you can use that rock for fill when you build the trestle."

Completely taken in by Rainbow's deception, Quan's eyes began to twinkle and a smile spread over his broad yellow face. "Big joke!" he said. "We use rock, all right!"

That was the way Rip wanted him to regard it. He knew Quan would quickly communicate that feeling to the others.

Mei-lang was not fooled by Rainbow's subterfuge and as they hastened across to the headquarters car, she said with frank annoyance, "You were only pretending to be pleased about this. Actually, you haven't any thought of laughing it off."

"No, I haven't," Rip admitted readily. "It's all the more reason for keeping the crew from getting jittery. That was my only purpose in speaking to Quan as I did. But I may not have been laying it on as thick as you think; if we play our cards right—and have a little luck—this night's business could help us more than it hurts. There's McCandless shouting to us!"

McCandless was stamping back and forth beside his car and paying little attention to the explanations for the explosion being offered him by his engineers, rodmen, and clerks. Grumpy stood on the car steps, unruffled by the excitement of the others. He had spoken his mind and he had nothing to add to it.

"Ripley, what do you make of this?" McCandless whipped out. "I think they had an accident up there—that the blast went off before they were ready. Your partner says I'm all wrong—that Slade intended to play it this way."

"I agree with him," Rainbow said flatly. "There wasn't anything premature about this blast. That gang must have been up on the mountain for a week, drilling. You may not have realized it, Mac, but Slade gave his hand away to-night. He was afraid to wait till you had the crew in there. He knew a score of men would be killed. That was too big an order for him; he knew he couldn't get away with it. He'll pull any trick to delay you. Maybe he's acting on orders from the party who's putting up the money for him. I don't know about that, but I can tell you for sure that Ben Slade is bluffing; he doesn't intend to face a murder rap."

"That's fine!" McCandless snorted sarcastically. "You talk as though we hadn't been hurt at all! How long do you think it's going to take me to clear up the mess he left me?"

"The better part of a week, I'd say. But you can use the rock. The time won't be a complete loss."

"And you think we won't be fired on when we go into the cut?"

The tall man had to call on his patience. "I don't think anything of the sort," he said quietly. "In fact, I'd almost guarantee that you'll run into gunfire. But if anyone gets hurt, it'll be an accident. Grumpy and I will pull out of here now and try to be up on the mountain by sunrise. Give us until noon. You go into the cut then; take just a man or two with you. If you don't lose your nerve, you'll be perfectly safe. When Grump and I get through with Slade's toughs, there won't be any more sniping from Split Rock."

The little one and he were saddled up and ready to ride in a few minutes. Rainbow managed a moment alone with Mei-lang.

"You're riding into danger," she said, not trying to conceal her fears for him. "It's happened so often before. I know it's useless to ask you to be careful."

"Don't worry," he pleaded. "This is routine with us. And don't forget it's Wyoming this fall, Mei-lang. I'll be planning and dreaming of it every day till you're there."

She gave him a last, long embrace and walked back to the cars. Rip turned to Grumpy. "Get aboard," he muttered soberly. "We'll ride!"

CHAPTER FIVE

SPLIT ROCK, when viewed from the construction camp, appeared to be an isolated peak; it was really the southern bastion of a broken mountain range that ran in a northwesterly direction all the way to the broken lava plateau below the Snake River. Though the partners' knowledge of the country north of the railroad was limited to what they had observed one afternoon, shortly after reaching Idaho, they had seen enough to convince them that the easiest way to reach the rim was to strike into the hills three or four miles above Split Rock and work back to it. But attempting it by night, and for the first time, made the going difficult.

"We're wearin' ourselves out for nothin'," Grumpy grumbled as it became apparent that the deep canyon into which they had ridden had no exit save the one by which they had entered. This was the third time they had been forced to turn back. "The sun will git up early. If you'll lissen to me, we'll climb out on that last ridge and stay there till we can see what we're doin'."

"We can hold up till dawn," Rainbow said. "Better do it right here; it's halfway comfortable. That wind up on the ridge was cutting through me like a knife."

They pulled the saddles off the horses and tried to make themselves comfortable for the rest of the night. But it was cold even here in the protected canyon, and without a blanket, sleep was impossible. Wood was at hand. They were not disposed to risk a fire, however. Grumpy got out his pipe. When he had it going, he pillowed his head on his saddle and drew up his knees. In that seemingly uncomfortable jackknife position, he settled down for the night. Rainbow was up and down a dozen times, trying to walk the chill out of his bones.

Daylight was a long time coming. Dawn was actually some minutes away when they began moving through the ground mist that had settled in the canyon during the night. The sun was up long before they reached the ridge. The wind had blown itself out and the morning air was keen and invigorating.

They estimated that they were not more than two and a half miles from the rim of Split Rock. Swinging to the west of the canyons that had trapped them during the night, they moved along, climbing steadily, passing from one rocky mountain meadow to the next and taking advantage of whatever cover offered.

Both men took it for granted that death lurked here for them and well could be the price of carelessness. Old hands at this business, they studied every innocent-looking clump of scrub trees and outcropping, being only too well aware of the grim secret that might be waiting there.

Their immediate objective was to find the trail that Slade and his men had been using. It seemed reasonable to believe that the gang had found a way to reach the rim by coming up the western slope. Grumpy, a good tracker, had been moving along in the lead for some time, when a long gulch got in his way. He swung around to the head of it, and what he saw there made him pull up.

"Here it is," he muttered, as Rainbow joined him. "I don't know how far this gulch runs down the slope, but they been comin' and goin' this way aplenty. Hoss tracks all over. Some of 'em right fresh, too."

He got down from the saddle and dropped to his knees.

"Was the trail used this morning?" Rip asked, his tone sharp and urgent.

"No, the tracks ain't that sharp. There was moisture enough up here this mornin' for a shod hoofmark to hold an edge. If that bunch went down, it was last night. They may still be layin' out on the rim."

"There's one way to find out," the tall man said tersely. "We can't have much more than a mile to go. We'll take our time about it."

He got out the glasses and studied the country ahead of them with painstaking care. A wide, shallow valley, barren save for a few gnarled cedars and a thinning carpet of stunted sage, ran all the way up to the crest. He could find no sign of movement anywhere.

Slade's trail could have been followed easily enough, but they turned their backs on it and swung sharply to the left until they were out of the valley before they began picking their way up to the rim. With only half a mile to go, they found a pocket in the rocks where the horses could be left. Over Grumpy's objections, they pulled their rifles out of the saddle boots and proceeded on foot.

"Leavin' the broncs may be all right," the little man grumbled, "but I never saw no sense in puttin' myself afoot till I knew what I was up against. For all we know, we may have this mountain to ourselves."

"You wouldn't care to bet on it, would you?" Rainbow inquired brusquely. "If someone is handed a surprise this morning, I aim to see that it isn't us."

Presently, they were moving ahead only a step or two at a time. A broken-off pinnacle, several hundred yards back from the rim, looked as if it could be scaled. Rip was convinced that if they could get to the top, they could command a view of the entire southern face of Split Rock.

"Let's try it," Grumpy volunteered. "But be careful where you step; that granite's rotten. And don't put your hand on a rattler; they like to coil up on little ledges like those and sun themselves."

Halfway up, he encountered a snake of tremendous girth. The temptation to blow its head off was strong, but he settled by picking it up with the muzzle of his rifle and hurling it off into space.

They reached the top without further incident. Below them, a hundred yards off to the right, they saw three men stretched out comfortably on the rim. Rainbow put the glasses on them at once.

"Miggles, Nate Flood, and Moss Santell," he said, identifying them easily. "No sign of Slade."

"Reckon he figgered there was no need for him to stick around. Those three boys can throw enough lead into the cut to keep the construction crew from gittin' any work done. That's the only reason they're up here."

Proof of it came a few minutes later when Miggles crawled gingerly to the edge of the rim and peered below. Sharp fractures in the rimrock showed where the wall had been blown down.

Rainbow glanced at his watch. It was only a few minutes past nine.

"What do we do now?" Grumpy inquired.

"Stay put for a few hours. I told Mac not to venture into the cut before noon. Why don't you lie down and catch up on some of the sleep you didn't get last night?"

"I got as much as you did!" the little man retorted irascibly. He always made a point of resenting any favors due to his advancing years. "Those gents may run out on us, Rip."

"No, they got grub and blankets. They expect to be up here some time." The tall man smiled soberly. "I reckon we'll change their minds about that."

The morning wore along. There was not a cloud in the sky, and the dazzling white sunshine searched out every nook and cranny on the barren mountain top. Slade's men, all unaware that they were being closely watched, began to move around impatiently on the rimrock, obviously finding the rocky shelf uncomfortably warm, with not a patch of shade as big as a man's hat anywhere.

From far to the east came the faint toot of a locomotive whistle. The partners could see a plume of smoke trailing off across the plains.

"That's the combination from Ogden," Grumpy said. "It's allus noon before she pulls in." He consulted his watch. " 'Leven thirty-five. Reckon we won't have to wait much longer for some action."

"Mac will go over his mail before he leaves camp," Rip reminded him. "There won't be anything doing for another thirty to forty minutes. There goes Miggles again, crawling out on the lip of the rim and taking a look below."

"Nobody down there," the little one muttered, a moment or two later, as Slade's man crawled back and joined the others.

Half an hour later, Miggles crawled out once more. This time, he turned immediately and beckoned for Flood and Santell to join him. The three conferred briefly and then spread out along the edge of the rimrock. Lying flat on their stomachs, they pushed their rifles out in front of them and trained their sights on the cut below. Ike shot first, taking careful aim before he squeezed the trigger. Flood and Santell fired then, and they were equally deliberate.

"By damn, you called the turn!" the little one grunted. "Those gents know where them slugs are goin' before they send 'em on their way!"

Rip nodded. "We'll do a little fancy shooting, too. You take care of Miggles; I'll tickle up Mr. Flood. Drop your slugs a foot or two behind them."

Grumpy checked himself in the act of throwing his gun to his shoulder. "Rip—what do you figger them *hombres* will do when we start throwin' lead?"

"I figure they'll run. They'll try to get to their horses in a hurry. They don't know what our game is, so they'll take it for granted that we're trying to knock them off."

"By grab, that's what we oughta do!" the little one growled. "Be good riddance!"

"No," Rainbow said flatly, "we want them alive—even if we have to chase them all the way to Mud Springs."

"Reckon that's about what we'll have to do! We don't know where they hid their hosses."

"We'll know as soon as they make a break for them," Rip said over his shoulder. His rifle cracked a moment later, and hard on the heels of that first shot, Grumpy's gun bucked angrily.

Miggles and his companions lay there in stunned surprise for a moment. But only for a moment; gunfire was something they could understand, especially when it was directed at them. In one startled movement, they jerked around and sprang to their feet. All three caught the glint of sunlight on the partners' rifle barrels; Santell and Flood ran; Ike Miggles, built of sterner stuff, flung up his gun and peppered the top of the pinnacle with half a dozen slugs before he bolted across the rimrock after the others.

Their horses were not far away, but they made no attempt to reach them. In fact, they went no farther than the low granite dike that formed a rocky parapet for the rim proper. It was not over ten feet high, but by hugging it, they were safely out of range from the peak and free to move along the dike unseen. This unexpected move completely turned the tables on the partners.

"We better get down from here in a hurry or we won't get down at all!" Rainbow ripped out in dismay. "They'll work around behind us and we'll be a couple of sitting ducks, waiting to be picked off!"

"Serves us right!" Grumpy snorted in his exasperation. "We knew we wasn't playin' with no tenderfoots!"

"Get moving!" Rip told him. "Go over that long outcropping and start dropping back to the broncs."

The little one was already on his way down the rock, risking his neck as he leaped from foothold to foothold. Reaching the base of the little peak, he darted for the outcropping, rolled over it, and flung himself down behind its protection, waiting for Rip to join him. But the seconds ticked away and Rip did not come. Throwing caution to the winds, Grumpy reared up and peered over the outcropping.

A glance confirmed his fears. Miggles and Santell had Rainbow pinned up against the foot of the peak, one edging up on his left, the other on his right. Both had their guns raised, ready to cut him down if he took a step With a savage snarl, Grumpy flung up his rifle and got Miggles in the sights, only to have Rip yell, "Look out, Grump! Behind you!"

The little man leaped aside, flinging his rifle away as he jumped. When he swung around, he had his .45 in his fist. Before he could bring it up, a slug pinged off the outcropping where he had been standing a moment before.

Thinking he had things his own way, and to get a better shot, Nate Flood had stepped out of an opening in the outcropping. No more than thirty yards separated the two men. At that distance, a rifle was not the fastest weapon. But he got in a second shot, and Grumpy felt the bullet's cold breath as it whined past his cheek. Unhurried, his eyes narrowed to slits in his hard-bitten face, he fired, and the old hogleg that he had carried so long and that had served him so well did not fail him now.

That slug raised Flood to his toes. He was a dead man even then, but before the young, lantern-jawed blackleg crumpled up, another bullet from the old Colt's crashed through him. Whipping around to shoot it out with Miggles and Santell, the little one was just in time to see them pulling back. He fired at Miggles but couldn't be sure he had hit him. In another moment or two, he heard them running.

"Come on!" Rainbow rapped. "We're going to need the horses now—and don't start yapping! I know that was a close call, and all my fault!"

He had never been angrier with himself. This was not the first time that a carefully thought out plan of his had backfired. What made the present instance so galling to him was knowing that he had played his hand badly; that whatever the cost, Grumpy and he should have jumped the three men when they were stretched out on the rim. But this was no time for recrimination. Beyond question, Miggles and Santell would lose no time now in quitting Split Rock. That they would take the trail down the gulch seemed equally certain. To get there first and either capture them or turn them back was Rip's thought.

The terrain at the head of the gulch was such that any hope of catching the men by surprise was out of the question. Confident that a few minutes' grace was theirs, the partners turned down the mountainside.

They had not proceeded far when the trail swung narrowly around a deep chasm.

"Pull up," Rip ordered. "We'll wait for them here; they'll be right on top of us before they spot us."

Grumpy took a look around and was satisfied they could not find a better place in which to jump Miggles and Santell. "There won't be any turnin' around here," he growled, peering below. "A pony makes a misstep and it's a goner." He glanced at Rainbow. The latter's mouth was tight and grim. "What's got you so worried?"

"We left a dead man up on top. If it hadn't been him, it would have been you—or both of us. You had to kill him, Grump. But that won't help us any with the sheriff. The fat's in the fire now; we'll either have to back him down or bow out of this scrap the best way we can."

"Good Christopher!" the little one screeched. "We better bow out and hang up our guns for keeps if we've got to the point where we gotta walk wide of a crooked sheriff and a skinflint judge! Let 'em turn loose their wolf! We'll show 'em he's got a loud bark and no teeth!" His voice shaking with fury, he added, "This is still the United States and Mustang Gap is a danged small part of it!"

Rainbow took it calmly. "I don't intend to walk wide of Lockhart or anybody else; I was just telling you that the chips are down. Better get set; Miggles and Santell will be showing up directly. If they cut down on us, bust them; we ain't pulling any punches now."

The two men rode down the gulch with a rush until they reached the chasm. They slowed their ponies to a walk then. The partners couldn't see them, but they heard them picking their way along the treacherous brink.

Ike Miggles rode in the lead. Santell was right behind him. When they caught their first glimpse of Rip and the little one, the latter were not ten feet away.

"Put 'em up!" Rainbow commanded.

"Go on—reach!" Grumpy supplemented.

The two men were too startled to do more than stare their amazement for a moment. Santell put his hands up then, and after debating the situation with himself, Miggles followed suit.

The little one swung down from the saddle and got their guns.

"We'll have to go down the slope ahead of you," Rainbow told them. "No room for passing here. If you've got any idea of making a break, forget it; it won't be healthy."

Santell took it in stony silence. Miggles hurled a curse

at Rip. "What yuh goin' to do with us?" he snarled, his rocky face contorted with rage.

"We're taking you into the Gap. Your friend Lockhart is going to have the unpleasant duty of locking you up."

"Yeh?" Miggles croaked scornfully. "Yuh won't make that stick; Slade will have us on the street before yuh have time to git turned around!"

"We'll see," Rip said softly. "Maybe Ben will be in the pokey, keeping you company before this is over. You can start moving. We'll stop at the construction camp before we head for town."

He sounded sure enough of himself, but in his mind there was the gravest doubt that any charge he brought against Slade and his blacklegs over what had occurred on Split Rock this morning, and the previous evening, would put them on the shelf even temporarily. He was determined, however, to play his hand for all it was worth.

The partners' arrival in camp with their prisoners created a stir. Rip walked aside with McCandless and gave him a full account of what had taken place on the mountain. The latter had news, too. He had gone into the cut with two of his men. One of them, Tom Hickman, an engineer, had been struck on the arm by a ricocheting bullet. The camp doctor had removed the slug from the man's arm.

"Good!" Rainbow exclaimed. "Now we've got something with teeth in it, Mac! All I saw ahead of us was to charge those men with trespassing and destroying property; we can make it assault with a deadly weapon now. The wound may be superficial, but it'll do. You put Hickman and the doctor in your buggy and drive into town. Grumpy will tag along with these birds. I'll go now. Give me about half an hour. When you hit town, come to the courthouse—the district attorney's office. I'll be waiting for you."

CHAPTER SIX

IT HAD NOT OCCURRED to Bemis Price, when he was elected district attorney, that he had got as far as he was going to go politically. He was a timid, nervous man, already balding, though still in his early thirties.

Lockhart had repeated to him what Rainbow had said about the Denver and Pacific lawyers being in Boise, conferring with the state's attorney general. The judge had heard it, too. He had scoffed at the veiled threat, but Price had taken it more seriously. Being a worrying man, he had not been able to put it out of his mind. He had used his office to further the plot against the railroad, and he knew that any investigation would reveal it.

The blast that ripped off great sections of the rim of Split Rock had not been heard in town, but ranchers living to the east had brought in word of a heavy explosion. Slade was in Mustang Gap. Judge Jarvis had sent for him and demanded and got an explanation. The judge relayed the information to the district attorney. The old man neither feared nor respected Price, and in his book fear and respect amounted to the same thing.

"It was a smart move," he said, as he was leaving. "It'll slow the work up for a week or more—and there's little or nothing the D. and P. can do about it. You just sit tight, Bemis. Don't do nothing till you consult me."

Sitting tight was not one of Bemis Price's accomplishments. He had never been convinced that any program of sabotage and delay would force the Denver and Pacific to change its plans and build through Mustang Gap. He had gone along with Jarvis because he believed that was the side of his bread on which the butter was to be found. It did no good to call himself a fool at this late last, but he knew he had gone as far as he wanted to go, and when Rainbow walked into the office, shortly after three o'clock, Bemis was deeply engrossed with trying to find a way out for himself. His worries multiplied as he listened to what his visitor had to say.

Pretending that this was the first he had heard of the dynamiting of Split Rock, Price said, "So that was the explosion Jim Foraker reported he'd heard, when he came in from his ranch up on the bench this morning. It's fortunate no one was injured."

"Very fortunate for Slade," Rip asserted. "You know that's state land along there. The D. and P. was granted a right of way, running back fifty yards on both sides of the track. That makes the southern face of the mountain railroad property. Slade and his men were there unlawfully. The mess they left will cost the company thousands of dollars to clean up. But that's not my personal concern; McCandless will handle that end of it. I'm concerned about what happened this morning."

He continued with a detailed account of what had taken place on the mountain. It brought the district attorney to the edge of his chair. Price wasn't acquainted with Nate Flood, but he had seen the man around town on numerous occasions.

"You were a witness to the shooting, Ripley?"

"I saw every bit of it. If I hadn't yelled when I did, my partner would have been shot in the back. As it was, Flood fired twice before the little fellow dropped him. You'll find the body up there. An examination of Flood's gun will verify what I'm telling you. There doesn't want to be any tampering with that evidence, Mr. Prosecutor."

Price reared up, shaking with indignation. "What do you mean by that remark?"

"That I know the score around here. I've got evidence enough right now to blow things wide open. You took an oath to enforce the law. I'm giving you a chance to do it before I go over your head."

Rip smiled thinly. He had made his estimate of the man across the desk and put him down for a lightweight.

Bemis Price had all he could do to contain himself. His face working nervously, he said, "That's pretty strong talk, Ripley! You can't come in here and threaten me!"

"Maybe it's a warning, rather than a threat," the tall man returned evenly. "You know Slade is a crook; that he's been engaged in criminal activities for years. Any man who befriends him, whether he be judge, prosecutor, sheriff, or dishwasher, lays himself open to suspicion. I know Ben Slade and all five of his gun slingers had a hand in this job. But I'll waive that point. I want warrants for the arrest of Slade, Ike Miggles, and Moss Santell. Miggles and Santell were caught dead to rights. I'm sure there can't be any question in your mind but what they were there carrying out Slade's orders."

"What's the charge?" Price demanded, drawing himself up stiffly in an attempt to recapture his dignity.

"Assault with a deadly weapon. One of our engineers was struck by a bullet from one of their guns. McCandless is bringing him in, as well as the camp doctor who dug the slug out of the man's arm. My partner will be showing up with them. He'll have Miggles and Santell in tow."

The day was not warm, but Price's face was so damp with perspiration that his glasses kept dropping off his nose. "You're going too far, Ripley!" he whipped out shrilly. "The sheriff warned you not to take the law into your own hands. You haven't the power of arrest!"

"Nobody's been arrested—yet," Rainbow said with maddening imperturbability. "We're leaving that to Lockhart. We just persuaded Miggles and Santell to come along. They'll be here directly. You better send for the sheriff. He can pick Slade up later."

Bemis popped out of his chair. "You wait where you are a few minutes; I'm going across the hall!"

He hurried out, slamming the door behind him. That he was bound for Judge Henry Jarvis's chambers was a certainty in Rip's mind. The tall man sat back, relaxed, confident that he had put his finger on the weak link in Slade's political setup.

The door to the judge's private room was closed. Price usually knocked before entering. But not today. Rushing in, he found Slade and Jarvis there. In his excitement, words tumbled from his lips and he was not stopped until he had told the whole story. Slade attempted to brush it all aside. "Take it easy, Bemis," he advised. "Nothin' will come of it."

Jarvis rapped angrily on his desk, his flinty calm gone. "You listen to me, Ben! I'll do the talking! I warned you many times if there was any bloodshed you were to make God-awful certain it couldn't be laid at your door. It's only a slug in the arm this time, but that man Ripley will make the most of it. With Flood lying dead up on Split Rock—Miggles and Santell rounded up at gun point before they could get away—what more evidence do you think Ripley and his partner need to tie this job on you?"

"What the hell!" Slade burst out hotly. "Five minutes ago you was tellin' me what a smart trick it was, blowin' down that rimrock!"

"Sure! Sure! But that wasn't good enough for you, you had to mix guns into it!" Jarvis bounced to his feet and slammed back and forth across the room. "It was just damned nonsense to think that Ripley and Gibbs could be laughed off; they didn't get their big reputation for nothing. I told Lockhart so yesterday."

"We've got to do something, Judge," Price said anxiously. "This is only a little headache now; we better stop it before it gets to be a big one."

This was better than Jarvis ordinarily expected from Bemis. "You're right," he declared heavily. "Sign the warrants Ripley wants and get hold of Lockhart."

"What!" Slade exploded. "You mean you're goin' to lock us up?"

"That's the smartest thing we can do," the old man snapped. "Lockhart can take Miggles and Santell into custody now; if you want to keep out of sight for a few hours, all right. You can turn yourself in this evening. I'll have the three of you brought up for arraignment tomorrow morning. You plead innocent. I'll fix bail, and you can go about your business. I want Miggles and Santell to plead guilty. I'll set their bail at twenty-five hundred dollars. That'll keep them locked up till they come to trial on Friday."

"What are you doin'—walkin' out on me?" Slade roared, leaping to his feet, his eyes flaming with fury.

The judge shook his head contemptuously and waved him back. "Why don't you use your head? If Price and I can give Ripley the idea that he's got us buffaloed and that we're willing to go along with him, it'll take the heat off you. I can bring your men to trial, fine 'em a hundred apiece and give 'em thirty days in the lockup. That won't hurt 'em. I'll give you a separate hearing. Your lawyer can ask for a postponement. I'll grant it and keep moving the case back until the whole thing has blown over. If we try to knock Ripley down, you know what he'll do? He'll have the railroad lawyers ask for a change of venue, and the case will be moved to some other county. God knows what would happen then! They wouldn't stop with a simple case of assault!"

Jarvis went back to his desk and sat down, breathing heavily. He was a frail man, and for medicinal purposes (or so he claimed) he always kept a flask of whisky in a drawer. He reached for it now, feeling he needed a stimulant. Under his heavy gray brows, his old eyes were bright with cunning.

"You get out of here, Ben," he said bluntly. "Bemis, go back to your office. You can handle Ripley and McCandless if you'll just listen to everything they've got to say. If an argument develops, all the better. Give in, but be hard to convince. I don't want you to scrape the floor. It wouldn't fool 'em."

"Okay," Bemis muttered unhappily. "What about Flood? How are we going to regard the killing?"

"We'll accept it as self-defense. You tell Lockhart to see me before he sits down with you. I'll tell him what he's to do."

Grumpy's arrival at the courthouse with Miggles and Santell, as well as the coming of McCandless and the others, had not gone unnoticed. The fact that the sheriff had been sent for hurriedly, as well as that Bemis Price had not left the building, though it was long past his usual time for leaving, lent weight to the rumors flying over town that something of moment was taking place.

The day's issue of the *Item* was just off the press, when Mark Wigg, the publisher, heard that there was a big gathering in the district attorney's office. Dropping everything, he slapped on his hat and headed for the courthouse, only to have to cool his heels for an hour before Lockhart came out with Miggles and Santell and led them away. When the partners stepped out into the hall a few minutes later, Wigg pounced on them.

Rainbow had no hesitancy in telling him what had taken place. At the end he added, "I wouldn't jump to any conclusions. I know this trouble is a long way from being over. Drop around to the hotel this evening, if you figure it's safe to be seen in our company."

He had persuaded McCandless to stay in the Gap for the night, that all three might be on hand when the sheriff brought the prisoners into court to be arraigned.

After supper, the partners were seated on the porch of the Idaho House, with McCandless and Wigg, when word went along the street that Ben Slade had just walked into the sheriff's office and been locked up.

Grumpy wagged his head incredulously. "There's a joker in this somewheres! That gent wouldn't have given himself up unless he was dang shore he wouldn't be in long."

McCandless turned to Rainbow. "What do you think it means, Rip?"

"I figure it's part of the act they're putting on for our benefit. I thought so this afternoon when Price and Lockhart got their signals crossed once or twice."

That wasn't the way Mustang Gap was taking it. The talk in the hotel barroom and among the men standing around on the sidewalk was all of Slade and the turn matters had taken. The tenor of it was that he had reached the end of his rope and that the fight with the D. and P. was over.

"They seem to say it with a feeling of relief," Wigg observed. "I don't believe any more than you gentlemen do that this is the end of the trouble; but judging by the reaction tonight, I'm sure the end could come quickly."

The partners and McCandless were in the courtroom the next morning when the judge took the bench. Slade had an attorney there, representing him, who asked the court for a separate hearing for his client. When Jarvis granted the request, Rainbow knew what was coming. Miggles and Santell pleaded guilty. The crowded courtroom voiced its surprise when bail was set at twenty-five hundred dollars.

As planned, Slade pleaded innocent. His bail was set at five hundred. His attorney posted the money with the clerk, and Slade walked out, a free man; Miggles and Santell were led back to their cells.

"There's your joker, Grump!" Rip muttered cuttingly. "Slade won't serve a day. After a couple postponements, he'll get a small fine and a suspended sentence. Let's get out of here before I blow up."

On the way back to camp, McCandless, astride a rented horse, took a more optimistic view of the proceedings than the partners. "Say what you will, you made that old goat on the bench pull in his horns. And that goes for young Price, too. They didn't dare to dismiss the charge as they've done in the past. I suppose we ought to post a couple men up on the mountain until we get through the cut."

"I don't think that will be necessary," Rainbow told him. "Split Rock won't give you any more trouble. I imagine it'll be a different story when you get to the big wash. When you start putting up the wooden cribbing for your trestle, look out for fire."

McCandless found a wire from Ambrose MacDonald, filed at Reno, Nevada, waiting for him. It was brief. "Will be in Mustang Gap Thursday morning. Meet me."

"I knew my message would catch up with him somewhere," said McCandless. "Thursday morning—that's day after tomorrow. I asked him to meet us in Lander. He must think pretty well of the idea of starting construction on the branch line or he wouldn't be coming up to the Gap."

Rainbow found the news encouraging. "If we can convince him that the job should be tackled at once, how long will it take him to get started, Mac?"

"It'll take time. A survey will have to be run, a right of way secured, material and men brought in—a commissary established—"

"It don't want to take too long if it's goin' to do us any good," Grumpy declared glumly. "I agree with what Rip said about the big wash. That's where the showdown will come."

CHAPTER SEVEN

LOCKHART AND A DEPUTY brought Flood's body down from the mountain the following morning. The partners chanced to see them. Contrary to Grumpy's conclusion, Slade spared the county the expense of burying the man.

McCandless had moved his crew and some heavy equipment into the cut and was clearing away the debris the blast had brought down. The Chinese seemed to have overcome their nervousness and their impassive yellow faces lit up with a confident, friendly grin when Rainbow rode among them. By nightfall so much had been accomplished that McCandless and his assistants could not refrain from expressing their satisfaction.

"Some of them don't weigh over a hundred and forty pounds," said Rip, "but no job's too tough for them. Give them half a chance and they'll come through for you."

McCandless chuckled. "I'm sure they will if I can only keep you around. I don't know what Miss Seng told those yellow boys about you, but now that they know who you are, you sure rate high with them."

The tall man smiled enigmatically. "They're a strange people. I don't pretend to understand them. They've been treated like cattle in this country. Treat them like human beings, and there's little they won't do for you."

Pursuant to Rip's request, Quan Jee, the labor boss, had picked three men to guard the camp by night. Cheng Bow, the youngest of the three, spoke surprisingly good English. The others, Lee Kee and Moy Kim, had only the usual "pidgin" at their command. The partners had spent an hour with them during the afternoon and found that the men could ride and handle a gun. Through Cheng Bow, Rainbow had explained what he wanted them to do. At the first suspicion of trouble, they were to notify him immediately.

At supper, Rip suggested that Cheng Bow, Lee Kee, and

Moy Kim be relieved of all other duties. "You can't expect them to be on their toes if they've been swinging a pick all day."

"I thought it was understood they were to be taken off the work crew," said McCandless. "I certainly don't expect them to work day and night. You'll be speaking to them this evening. Tell them that patroling the camp from now on is all they'll be asked to do. You might mention it to Quan Jee, too."

Cheng Bow and his companions, already feeling that they had been signally honored by being selected from so many, and mounted and armed, were further pleased to learn that watching over the camp was all that was to be asked of them.

Though the partners were of the opinion that Slade would not make another move for a few days, they went out several times during the night with Cheng Bow and the others. Just before turning in, they rode back along the finished construction for several miles by themselves.

"This is far enough," the tall man said at last. "I'm going to leave you to look after things tomorrow; I'll go into the Gap with Mac and see what we can get out of MacDonald. He may feel we haven't accomplished very much."

"Is that so?" Grumpy snorted acrimoniously. "He better not try to sing that tune to me. We've done all right; things look a lot better than they did when we got here."

"No argument about that," Rainbow agreed, "but they'd look even better if we had a line on who is putting up the money for Slade. If we could put a finger on him, chances are we could break up this game in a hurry."

"It would help," the little one conceded. "I heard you sounding Wigg out. He couldn't tell you anythin'?"

"No, and it went a long way toward convincing me that it isn't any local party. In fact, it wouldn't surprise me if he'd never set foot in Mustang Gap. Figure it out for yourself, Grump. Some smart operator gets tipped off that the Denver and Pacific is going to build through this part of Idaho. He looks at a map and sees the road has a branch line running up from Nevada. The Gap is the only town of any size in this country. Wouldn't it be enough to convince him that quick money could be made if he bought some cheap land?"

"Yeh, that sounds all right; but why don't he move in himself? Why does he hire Ben Slade to handle things?"

"I've thought of that," said Rip. "Suppose it was Slade who tipped him off and cut himself in on the strength of what he knew? That might explain it. I can think of two or three other reasons why a crook with a bankroll might find it advisable to keep under cover."

They continued to discuss the matter as they moved back to camp.

"I'd like to see Slade's bank account," Grumpy remarked. "If he's receivin' checks or drafts, the bank records would show where they come from."

"We haven't the authority to compel the bank to show us its books, Grump. The post office would be a better bet. You can be sure Slade and his backer are in touch with each other, and they're no doubt doing it by mail. But there again we'd be stopped; the post office doesn't hand out any information, short of a court order. Ben's got an old roll-top desk in his office. It was locked when I was up there the other morning. If we could go through it, we'd find what we want to know."

"Yeh, and if we got caught, that old goat Jarvis would throw the book at us and we'd wind up in the Idaho pen for a year or two. There's one thing you can do tomorrow, Rip. Speak to the railroad agent in the Gap. He must know Slade by sight. Find out if Ben has been runnin' down to Lander. If he has, we can be dang sure that that's where he's gittin' together with his side-kick."

"I'll do that," Rainbow replied. "It's a good idea."

The night passed without incident, and in the morning Rip and McCandless left for town right after breakfast. For all of their early start, they still had some miles to go when the Lander local, with little Ambrose MacDonald's private car attached, pulled into the Gap. This was the first time that one of the Denver and Pacific's high brass had honored the place with his presence.

Ambrose had breakfasted already, and while the train was being switched around for the afternoon run back to Lander, he stepped down on the platform to stretch his legs, looking the depot and trackage over as carefully as though he were only a division superintendent on an inspection trip.

Virgil Barnum, the company's local agent, had learned from the conductor that the visitor was Ambrose MacDonald, Assistant to the President of the D. and P. System. He was so flabbergasted by the great man's presence that when MacDonald came up to the ticket window and introduced himself, he tipped his cap and had difficulty pronouncing his own name.

"Has anybody from the construction camp been in this morning asking for me, Mr. Barnum?"

"No, sir, I ain't seen no one at all," Virgil told him, his old upper plate clacking noisily with every syllable.

"I'm going to walk up the street and look the town over," said Ambrose. "There'll be someone here asking for me. If they show up before I get back, tell them to wait."

Virgil wanted to warn him that there was so much feeling against the railroad in Mustang Gap that it might be just as well for him not to show himself. But he couldn't find the courage to say anything and he stood at the window scratching his head impotently as the little man strode away briskly.

Word that a railroad official had arrived in his private car had set the Gap to buzzing. Little Ambrose surmised as much. But hostile towns had never frightened him, and he met the unfriendly attention he attracted this morning with a flinty contempt. He was on his way back to the depot when Rainbow and McCandless drove past. The latter blinked on catching sight of him and pulled up his team. "Ambrose," he scolded, "don't you know it's open season around here on anyone connected with the D. and P.?"

"Tut! Tut!" MacDonald scoffed, removing the unlit

cigar from his mouth. "I've been enjoying myself." Nodding to Rip, he said, "I'm glad to see you. I'll get in the back seat and ride down to the car with you."

Barnum saw them coming. He knew McCandless by sight, but this was the first time he had seen Rainbow. Ambrose made them acquainted. The tall man asked Virgil about Slade.

"I've had him pointed out to me," Virgil told him. "I can't recall him using the road. If he'd been going back and forth between the Gap and Lander, I'd have spotted him, whether he bought a ticket or not."

"That's all I wanted to know," said Rip.

"You sound disappointed," MacDonald remarked as they crossed the tracks to his car. "Something important?"

"Not particularly. It just rules out an idea that occurred to my partner."

McCandless's daily report to the company's Denver offices, detailing his progress, or lack of it, had passed across Ambrose MacDonald's desk, so the latter wasn't unfamiliar with what had been happening. Nevertheless, he had so many questions that the morning was half gone before the subject was exhausted. In his incisive way, he said, "The skies look somewhat brighter, but as of this morning, we are still dropping further and further behind schedule. By now we should have steel laid all the way to the Oregon line." He turned to Rainbow. "I didn't expect you to pull a rabbit out of the hat," he continued. "I felt sure you and your partner would do a job for us. Knowing what you're up against, I must say I'm well satisfied with what you've accomplished. In fact, I wish we had sent you out here weeks ago. I understand from Mac that this idea of driving the stub line up to the junction at once originated with you."

"Not quite," Rainbow replied. "The editor of the local paper suggested it to me. I know it will help us tremendously. It'll cut Slade's support away from him and put him out on the end of the limb."

Little Ambrose nodded in complete agreement. "It's an excellent idea, no matter who first thought of it. The only question in my mind is how best to handle it. I don't want to pile any more work on you, Mac."

"What about O'Mara?" McCandless asked. "Can't you pull him off the Colorado job and ship him out here with his crew? Fifteen miles—that won't take him long. It's practically flat country. Rip and I looked it over carefully this morning. That's why we were late getting in. A right of way to the east of the county road that runs north out of Mustang Gap would get us there with only three or four cheap fills and little or no blasting. Time is precious, Ambrose. Hustle somebody out from our land department. They all can't be busy. I can spare men to run the survey."

"Leave it to me," MacDonald told him. He made some notes in the little black book that he always carried in his vest pocket. "I'll have a contract man here by Monday. By the middle of next week, men and material will be rolling into Mustang Gap. We've got enough steel and ties piled up at our Nevada division points to take care of this job. Who will you put in charge of the surveying?"

"I'll let you have Con Hughes. He's the best I've got."

"Fine—if you can spare him. Talk things over with Con; show him what we want. See that he's here Monday morning. You'll have a wire before then, telling you who they're sending out. I'm going to ask for Grundy." MacDonald pulled out his watch. "Eleven-twelve," he said. "I've got a good cook with me this trip. If you gentlemen don't mind having an early lunch, I'll tell him to get something started. The southbound is due to pull out at one-o-five. If we're not finished, I'll hold the train up a few minutes."

Rainbow and McCandless accepted his invitation, and after the chef had been called in and given some instructions, they continued their conversation.

"I'd like to make a suggestion," said Rip. "Unless we're all badly mistaken, the company's decision to build up to the junction at once will stand this town on its head. The sooner the news breaks, and the more publicity it gets, the better. Why not get the editor of the *Item* down here, Mr. MacDonald, and give him the story? He'll give

Mustang Gap something to talk about over the supper table tonight."

Ambrose MacDonald put the tips of his fingers together as he pondered his answer. "If we let the cat out of the bag, it will cost us more to acquire a right of way. But it might be worth while at that. Publicity pays dividends as well as anything else. Suppose you get him, Ripley."

The Lander train had been gone for several hours and Rainbow and McCandless were back in camp by the time the *Item* came off the press that afternoon. Under a five-column head it screamed the news that the Denver and Pacific Railroad was to start building north at once. Mustang Gap rocked under its impact. At the courthouse, it sent Bemis Price flying across the hall to the judge's chambers. Gid Penny, the town marshal, hurried into the sheriff's office and shoved a copy of the paper into Lockhart's hands. It took Lockhart approximately two minutes to read the news. Gulping his surprise, he pushed Gid out of the way and headed for the courthouse, looking like a man who has just had the rug pulled out from under him.

Slade was upstairs in his office, writing a letter, when Pete Cleary and Joe Fanin clumped up the stairs with a copy of the *Item*. They now formed a minority of two of the five worthies he had brought to the Gap to do his bidding.

"Ben, take a look at this!" Cleary grunted. "You wondered what that little gent in the private car was doin' in the Gap, and why Ripley was sent up for Mark Wigg. Here it is, all spelled out for you!"

Slade snatched the newspaper away from him and read the article aloud. Finished, he slammed the paper on his desk. "I don't believe a damn word of it!" he bellowed. "This is some more of Mark Wigg's lyin'! That dirty, meddlin' pup cooked up the whole thing!"

"Reckon that ain't the way Jim Lockhart figgers it," Cleary told him. "We just saw him high-tailin' it up the street for the courthouse. That big Adam's apple of his was jumpin' up and down his throat like he was tryin' to swaller it."

"Is that so? I'll tell Jarvis and the rest of 'em where they get off!" Grabbing his hat, Slade slammed down the stairs.

As he expected, he found Price and Lockhart closeted with the judge. He greeted their long faces with a mocking laugh. Before he could speak, the judge said, "Sit down!"

Slade caught a chair with his boot and pulled it over to him. "What the hell is this, a funeral? You goin' to let Wigg throw you with the junk he dreamed up? I tell you there's nothin' to it!"

He was only talking for their benefit. He knew what the score was as well as they did; but their allegiance was vital to him; he had to keep them in line. Lockhart turned on him hotly.

"Ben, that's the dumbest thing I ever heard you say! You'll find there's plenty to it. You know as well as we do that MacDonald was in the Gap this mornin'—that Ripley and Dan McCandless knew he'd be here and came in to meet him. You know they had Wigg down to the car. Don't try to tell us they was gittin' together to discuss the price of beef!"

"Have it your way," Slade conceded sarcastically. "So it's all true. So what?"

To the surprise of all, Bemis Price popped to his feet, his timidity gone. "I'll tell you so what!" he cried, shaking an accusing finger at Slade. "By tomorrow morning there won't be a corporal's guard left in this town who'll go to bat for you or give a tinker's damn about where the Denver and Pacific goes through to the Coast. All four of us are out on the end of a limb, and you better get that through your head."

"That's right!" Lockhart grunted. "It ain't necessary to go into the reasons; it's enough to say you've had things yore own way around here. Now that folks has got a part of what they wanted, they'll change their tune; they won't stand for any more of the stuff we let you git away with. If we try it, we'll be finished, come election time."

That was what Bemis Price feared. He had seen the so-called handwriting on the wall when Rainbow had demanded warrants for Slade, Miggles, and Santell. It had taken this present turn of affairs, however, to get his eyes really open.

"Wait a minute, Ben!" Jarvis interjected as Slade was about to explode. "Losing our tempers won't help any of us. If we have any brains, this is the time to use them. Let's discuss this matter calmly." He had seen the light, too, and was as anxious as Bemis and Lockhart to get out from under. "There isn't a retail establishment in town that won't profit in some way out of this decision to start building the branch line. That's almost as important to the Gap as the fact that we ain't going to be left high and dry at the end of a stub line. The railroad company will bring in a big crew of men. They'll have to be fed. They'll buy shoes, boots, socks, overalls, and everything else a man needs. Anyone with a team will find work for his horses And the saloons—they'll reap a harvest! Those are things we got to face."

"Yeh!" Slade snarled. "And you can face the fact that you got some land north of town. You'll be sellin' a nice piece of it to the railroad. That's in the back of your mind, too, ain't it?"

The old man eyed him coolly. "I could give you a better answer if I knew where the junction is to be located and how they're going to get there. I own a little land just west of the Gap. If I get my price, I'll unload it, same as you'd do. Is there anything wrong with that?"

"You got a crust, sittin' there askin' me if there's any thin' wrong with a deal that leaves me holdin' the bag!" Across the desk, Slade's heavy face was rocky with rage "You're kiddin' yourself if you think I'm licked! I can play it alone if I have to!"

"That's up to you," Jarvis said, with a stony lack of inflection. "Just remember this—from now on you'll be responsible to the law. You and your two boys are coming up for trial tomorrow morning on the assault complaint I'll handle it as I said I would. But that's as far as I can go, Ben."

CHAPTER EIGHT

MUSTANG GAP WAS FINDING the Denver and Pacific's decision to build north at once far more interesting than the outcome of the trial; and when Slade walked into the courtroom with his lawyer a few minutes after Lockhart and a deputy arrived with Miggles and Santell, it was not half filled.

The partners had reached town well ahead of McCandless and his party. The absence of excitement at the courthouse struck them at once. Overnight the atmosphere of Mustang Gap seemed to have changed; the tension was gone from the air.

"How do things look?" McCandless inquired, when he met them on the courthouse steps. He had Con Hughes, his chief engineer, with him, as well as the camp doctor and Hickman.

"They're working out just as we expected," said Rip. "Yesterday's announcement has broken the back of the opposition to the company. I don't know what effect it will have on Jarvis. We figured he'd hand out some light fines and that that would be the end of it."

"Don't git yore expectations up too high," Grumpy declared pessimistically. "Ben Slade ain't goin' to jail this mornin'. Let's go in."

The proceedings took only a few minutes. Price read the indictment against Miggles and Santell. They admitted their guilt and were fined a hundred dollars each and sentenced to thirty days in the county jail. When Slade's turn came, he went to the bar with his attorney. The latter asked for a postponement, and Jarvis granted it without argument. That was all.

"What did I tell you?" Grumpy grumbled as the little group from the camp filed out of the courtroom. "Slade was the party we wanted put out of circulation. The whole thing was cut and dried!"

"I'm sure it was," Rainbow agreed. "But we got half a loaf, and that's better than nothing."

McCandless had given Hughes his idea of where the right of way north from the Gap should run. With a couple of rodmen, Con ran a preliminary survey on Saturday and Sunday and was in town Monday morning to meet Alex Grundy of D. and P.'s land department. They went to the county clerk's office and learned who owned the land they wanted. By nightfall, everyone in the Gap knew where the Lander division was to be placed and where it was to meet the new mainline to the Coast. Though the prices asked for the land were high, coming to terms with the owners was not difficult, for Grundy had been instructed that time, rather than money, was of the essence. Even so, flat cars laden with steel and ties were being shunted upon the Mustang Gap siding before the last contract was signed.

Out at camp, the Chinese crew was proving what it could do when it could work without molestation. The cut had been cleared and roadbed was being graded well beyond Split Rock. Timbers for the cribbing that was to form the trestle across the big wash had begun to arrive. In the wash itself, masons were constructing drainage pipes.

When Grumpy had expressed his conviction that the showdown with Slade would come in the dry wash, Rainbow found himself of the same opinion. Recent events had supplied him with additional reasons for believing it.

Physically, the wash resembled a thirty-foot-deep ditch, an eighth of a mile wide, the bottoms clogged with dry brush and dead willows and providing a lurking enemy with excellent cover. A wide swath would be cleared across the wash before work started on the cribbing; but even though the brush and scrub were piled up and burned, acres of equally inflammable material would remain. It could be ignited easily. Once set ablaze it could, with the help of a favoring wind, soon have the wash in flames from bank to bank. A roaring fire of such proportion would not be halted by the clearing; the flames would leap across and make a flaming torch of the cribbing.

For the past several days, the partners had been riding out to the wash every afternoon. Accompanied by Cheng Bow, they were there again today. Rainbow had asked the young Chinese to ride with them. He was already planning how the trestle was to be guarded, and he wanted to explain what he had in mind to Cheng. The latter listened to him with grave attention as they stood at the edge of the wash.

"We won't be getting down there for another week," said Rip, "but it's not too soon to begin thinking about what we're going to do. I don't believe there's any question but what an attempt will be made to burn us out."

"I understand," said Cheng. "Fire will be the great danger."

"Fire, mixed up with some bushwhackin', I reckon," Grumpy observed soberly. "If you boys don't keep yore eyes open, you'll ride into trouble down there some night and not know it till guns start spittin' lead at you."

"I'm afraid that's true," said Rip. "We'll be down there with you."

"You and me can be knocked off as well as anybody else," the little one persisted grimly. "Slade knows it will be his last chance to slow up the work; he'll be so desperate he won't stop at nothin'. Nobody but us will have any business down there after nightfall."

Rainbow gave him a sharp, probing glance. "You seem to have something on your mind. What is it?"

"Jest this; make it plain to Cheng that we shoot first and ask questions later."

"There's no other way for us to play it," the tall man agreed without hesitation. "I thought it was understood." Turning to Cheng, he said, "I want you to be sure on that point. You've seen Slade often enough in town to know him. How about the others—Pete Cleary and Joe Fanin?"

"I know who they are," Cheng said softly. "So do Lee and Moy."

On the way back to camp they saw a score of laborers chopping sagebrush to the west of the cut and getting ready to lay an ungraded siding. In the cut itself, a locomotive was carefully pushing a loaded flat car over the newly laid rails.

"You know what that means," Grumpy remarked, indicating the siding with a jerk of his head. "New camp. Wonder when we'll be movin' up?"

"Day after tomorrow Mac told me," Rip replied.

McCandless called them over to his car as they rode in. "I've got news for you, and it's purty hard to swallow. I was in town this afternoon; Grundy wanted to see me. He's got everything signed up. O'Mara and his Irishmen are rolling across Nevada right now. They should hit Mustang Gap sometime late tomorrow."

Puzzled, the tall man said, "What's wrong with that?"

"Rip, Grundy paid some fancy prices for the land he bought. Who do you think got most of the money?"

"I don't know—"

"Henry Jarvis."

"What!" Grumpy screeched. "You mean to say we played right into the hands of that old goat?"

"Seems we did," McCandless admitted ruefully.

Rainbow shared their chagrin, but the situation had its ironic humor, too, and he recognized it with a laugh. "This is what they call adding insult to injury, I reckon. Jarvis has played Slade's game from the start—done everything he could to tie you up, Mac; and now we shove a potful of gold into his hands. I wonder how Ben Slade feels about it?"

"By Christopher, I hope it slays him!" the little one growled. "I'd like to see that pair tear into each other!"

"They may, at that," Rip declared thoughtfully. "If they don't, I wouldn't give a nickel for our chances of getting across the wash without smelling gun smoke."

The big camp had been moved so often that a routine had been evolved and the operation could now be completed in a few hours.

After breakfast on the following morning, all but one, the cook and commissary tents were pulled down and stowed away on the waiting flats. The old Pullmans and made-over boxcars that housed the crew were already moving through the cut. The temporary sidings on which they had stood were torn up. The corrals for the livestock had been dismantled, to be put up again at the new camp. Horses, mules, wagons, and equipment had been the first to go. By noon, only piles of empty tin cans and rubbish remained to say that the camp had ever stood there.

With equal dispatch and absence of confusion, O'Mara had begun operations in Mustang Gap, with half the town out to watch his swaggering Irishmen, supplemented by several score of local men, go to work. For the asking, any able-bodied man who could swing a sledge or use a pick and shovel had a job, and at better wages than the town offered. That was doubly true of the pay offered anyone who had a team of horses heavy enough to handle a scraper.

A steam shovel made short work of cutting away the little sand hill just beyond the depot. When that barrier was removed, the way was open to the north, with the right of way following Mustang Creek until it was well beyond the town limits.

Ben Slade was not among the spectators. All this activity and excitement was nauseating to him. He refused to talk about it, let alone witness it. Utterly disgusted by the turn of events, he sulked in his shabby office, with Cleary and Fanin to keep him company and listen to his venom. Though he refused to admit it, he knew the Gap, where once he had been so strong, was no longer with him; Cleary and Fanin were all he had left, and even their allegiance was dubious.

The fancy price the judge had received for the worthless acreage he had sold to the railroad had been bitter medicine for Slade to take. He knew Jarvis, Bemis Price, and Lockhart were eager to make the break with him final and complete; that they held off only because they feared he might reveal that they had been paid for the services they had previously rendered him. He had refrained from doing it only because he knew he couldn't pull them down without making himself liable. But the bitterness of his feeling about them was as nothing compared to the black hatred he bore the partners. He held them responsible for the turn his affairs had taken. No matter what else happened, he was determined to even his score with them.

"We goin' to stick around town till Ike and Santell git out of the can?" Cleary asked.

"No, we ain't," was Slade's surly answer. "We'll buy some grub this afternoon and pull out for Mud Springs. It'll put us in a few miles of the big wash. If we hole up there and drop out of sight for a few days, mebbe Ripley and the little jerk will get curious and come lookin' for us."

"They won't have no trouble findin' the Springs." Cleary didn't like the idea and his tone expressed his displeasure. "We know they been in there before."

"That's what I'm countin' on," Slade growled. His meaning was clear enough. "I was doin' all right till that pair showed up. I've taken all I'm goin' to take from those gents!"

Cleary was not impressed. "What's it goin' to git us, knockin' them off?" he demanded, his narrowed eyes cold and hostile in his rocky face. "What sort of an out is it goin' to leave us?"

"I ain't lookin' for an out!" Slade rifled back fiercely. "And you get this straight, Pete, you ain't tellin' me where to head in! You been makin' a lot of cracks around here this mornin', and I don't like it, understand?"

Cleary prided himself on his toughness and in the present company he felt he could take care of himself. With a contemptuous shrug, he said, getting to his feet, "Nobody's askin' you to like it, Ben."

It was too much for Slade. Leaping out of his chair, he sent a fist crashing into Cleary's jaw. It was a wicked, staggering blow that made the man's knees buckle. Before he could throw off its effects, Slade caught him with a long, whistling right hand that sent him sprawling to the floor. He lay there with blood trickling from his mouth.

Fanin's sympathies were with Pete, but he stayed where he was, his eyes dark with his thinking, and said not a word as Slade reached down, wrapped his hand in the neck of Cleary's shirt, and dragged him to his feet. Drawing his fist back to hit him again, he changed his mind and flung him into a chair.

The big man stood there, taking a moment to catch his breath. "All right, Pete!" he grunted. "You pull yourself together. You and Joe go down to Kinder's and buy some bacon and coffee and enough other stuff to keep us goin' for a week. And don't you get no more funny ideas, understand!"

Cleary nodded and wiped his bruised mouth with the back of his hand. "Okay, Ben," he mumbled. "Okay—"

Slade gave them some money, and they went out. He sat at his desk after they had gone, brooding over his ill luck. He could find no comfort in his thoughts, no matter where they turned.

He pulled himself to his feet and walked to the window. He was in time to see the judge stepping into the bank. Sight of Jarvis swept him into a fit of uncontrollable rage. "You miserable, double-crossin' rat, you did all right for yourself!" he snarled. "I'd a done all right for myself, too, if I had followed your advice and taken things easy! I'm playin' it my own way now, and I'll make you like it!"

CHAPTER NINE

FOR SEVERAL DAYS McCandless had most of his crew cutting and burning brush. By the time the way had been cleared for the trestle, steel had been laid to the brink of the big wash. Immediately, a heavy mobile crane began lowering timbers for the cribbing.

The partners spent many hours scouting the wash without encountering anyone. It failed to shake their conviction that the progress of the work was being watched.

"I use binoculars and I imagine Slade is using them, too," Rainbow said one morning, as they were starting out. "From any of those low hills off to the west, he could get a bird's-eye view of what is going on."

"We could ride those hills today and have a look around," Grumpy suggested.

Rip said no. "Slade's got as much right to be there as we have. The only way we could run them out would be with gunfire. I've got a hunch that that's what he wants us to try. When he and his men pulled out of the Gap the other day, they were careful to let it be known they were heading for Mud Springs. They could have slipped away without saying anything. The talk had some purpose, Grump."

They rode the wash all day, and it proved as fruitless as others had until late in the afternoon. In past years, flash floods, following cloudbursts, had torn down the wash, piling up great mounds of dead scrub, sage, and buckbrush that needed only a lighted match to set them to blazing.

In turning off to avoid one such barrier, Rip and the little one were electrified to find fresh horse tracks in the powder-dry earth. With guns drawn, they circled around the piled-up brush. The tracks made the circle with them. Turning away, the partners reconnoitered the immediate vicinity. When they had assured themselves that no lurking enemy was waiting to cut them down, they returned to examine the tracks.

"They ain't more'n an hour or two old," the little one declared soberly. "We almost ran into somethin', Rip."

"Yeh," the tall man acknowledged quietly. He was looking things over carefully. "This pile of brush interested him, and I reckon we know why; it isn't far from where the trestle will stand– Let's follow his trail and find out how he got in here."

The animal that made the tracks had moved at a walk, and every impression his hoofs left was sharp enough to be easily followed.

The trail led north, and before it began to cut across to the west bank of the wash, the partners were fully three miles above the railroad. They went on until they found the spot where the rider had sent his horse up the bank.

"No use going any farther," said Rip. "It was Slade, or one of his men, and very likely Slade. What we should have done—and days ago—was to set this stuff afire ourselves. It's all waste land; fire couldn't have damaged anyone. It might have run down the wash for four or five miles, but on a still day, without any wind to fan the flames, it wouldn't have moved too fast. And we could always have backfired against it, if necessary."

"By Joe, that's still a good idea!" Grumpy exclaimed enthusiastically. "It ain't too late."

"Maybe it isn't," Rainbow replied. "We'll speak to Mac this evening. It would tie a knot in Ben Slade's tail."

McCandless shook his head when they sounded him out after supper. "I certainly won't okay any program like that," he said flatly. "We've got some of the cribbing up already, and there's better than five carloads of timbers and heavy lumber in the wash. Set things to blazing and I'll lose every stick of it. If you'd brought this up a week or two ago, I wouldn't have been for it. Start a fire of that size going and you can't be sure what will happen. Everybody tries to get something out of a railroad. I've seen juries award damages even when the point at issue had less merit than burning off a few hundred acres of scrub."

Rainbow did not attempt to argue the matter. He appreciated the reasons McCandless had advanced in making his decision and realized it would be useless to say anything further.

"You boys going into the wash tonight?" McCandless asked.

"For a few hours," said Rip. "It's a cinch Slade won't make his move until he can hurt you more than is possible right now. He can burn you out only once, Mac. Is it still your intention to complete the trestle before you begin with the fill?"

"Naturally. It's the only way the job can be handled economically." McCandless knocked the dottle from his pipe and reached for his tin of tobacco. "You may not have noticed," he added, with a wry smile, "but I've reached the point where I've got to save time and money."

"You won't do either if your trestle goes up in smoke some night and you have to do the job all over. That can happen, no matter what precautions we take."

McCandless's mouth tightened and there was no mistaking his annoyance. "I've given the two of you a free hand and taken your advice on a good many things. But this is a construction problem. You'll have to let me handle it my way."

"I'm sorry if I spoke out of turn," Rip said apologetically. "I wasn't trying to tell you your business, Mac. I never built a trestle and wouldn't know where to begin. My thought was that it might be possible to take some of the gamble out of the job."

"How? I'm no dog in the manger; I'll listen."

"Couldn't you complete fifty to sixty feet at a time—lay your rails and push your dump cars out on them and make your fill? You intend to build a short spur to the side of Split Rock and get your earth fill there. As for rock, you've got tons of it lying around. Couldn't that spur be built now as well as later? If you get burned out, the most you can lose will be a section of cribbing. Fire can't burn back beyond the end of the fill."

McCandless smoked his pipe thoughtfully for several minutes. Finally he said without prejudice, "It could be done. I'd have men crawling over one another for the first few days. But a little planning would take care of that."

"Sleep on it," Rip suggested.

"I intend to. I'll put it up to the staff and my foremen in the morning. All the lumber I've got down there would have to be moved back before we started the fill. That'll be a job in itself."

"But it'll be safe when you git it moved," Grumpy asserted. "The prevailin' wind in the wash is from the north. Move everythin' to the south of the fill and no fire will reach it."

Following an early-morning conference, the plan Rainbow had advanced was put into effect. It resulted in some confusion, but after a day or two the work went ahead smoothly, if not as rapidly as before.

Slade was keeping a careful watch on the building of the trestle. The work was not proceeding as he had expected, and by the end of the week, he realized that the moment for which he had been waiting would never come.

"No question about it," he complained across the breakfast campfire to Cleary and Fanin at Mud Springs. "I figured we'd let 'em finish the cribbin', then burn down the whole damn works. But they ain't goin' to build it that way; they're finishin' a few feet at a time."

"Yo're runnin' things, Ben," Cleary muttered, with a disinterested shrug. "We can always set the brush on fire. It'll hurt 'em some."

"To hell with that!" Slade snarled. "I wanted to stop them cold!"

"Mebbe you can, at that," Fanin spoke up. He seldom had anything to say; that little, however, usually made sense. "They got thousands of dollars worth of pine and Oregon spruce piled up in there. Carloads of it. If they lose it, work will stop for a few weeks."

Slade shook his head. "A brush fire won't reach it, Joe. The wind's from the wrong direction."

"It is in the evenin'. About an hour before dawn it blows the other way. I been in the wash every night for a week, and that dawn wind has always been right on time.

For thirty, forty minutes, it blows right smart."

"Good!" Slade jerked out, visibly enthused. "It'll do the trick! I'll go in with you boys tonight and we'll touch things off."

"What about Ripley and his pardner—and those three Chinamen?" Cleary asked. "They're in the wash all night. We're sure to bump into some of 'em."

"Don't worry about the Chinks, Pete. They'll run at the first sign of trouble. If Ripley and Gibbs come at us, we'll have to shoot it out. And we better be damn sure we shoot first! We'll go in a couple miles above the trestle. I was in there the other day and had a good look around. When the north wind starts to drop, we'll set the brush afire and move down the wash as quick as we can."

Fanin and Cleary understood what Slade expected that trick to accomplish. The latter, characteristically, shook his head dubiously as he considered its chances of accomplishing its purpose.

"The blaze will draw their attention that way," he argued, "but it won't stampede Ripley and his side-kick; they'll stick close to the trestle. When we start movin' down the wash, they'll spot us and there'll be a helluva fight. Why not send one man up there? It ain't goin' take more'n two of us to go after that pile of timbers."

To Cleary's surprise, Slade said, "Pete, you got somethin' there! You go in up above; Joe and me will handle the rest of it. We'll meet back here at the Springs by sunup."

The partners had worked out a routine for patrolling the wash. Since it was their conviction that the likelihood of trouble was far greater from above, they policed the northern fringe of the clearing themselves, one moving across the wash from east to west and the other from west to east and meeting every fifteen minutes to exchange a word or two. Below them, Cheng Bow, Lee Kee, and Moy Kim followed the same procedure, with all five men keeping well back in the brush, thus lessening the chances of their being picked off by a sniper.

This night began as so many others had, without anything happening, and it was after three in the morning, when Rip and the little one pulled up alongside each other for a few minutes. After parting, they had not put more than several yards between them when a telltale redness in the sky turned them around and brought them together again.

"This is it!" Grumpy cried. "That's fire, and she's beginnin' to roar!"

"There's nothing we can do about it," Rainbow said phlegmatically. "We'll stay right where we are as long as we can. Whoever set this blaze may be moving down the wash. If you see anyone running, drop him."

The fire spread swiftly. In a few minutes the brush was ablaze from bank to bank, the flames leaping forty to fifty feet into the air. Clouds of acrid white smoke blotted out the sky. Windborne ashes showered down on the aroused camp. It was a thrilling, awesome spectacle.

"By damn, I reckon Mac's thankin' his lucky stars he listened to you!" Grumpy ground out. "If he had his trestle standin', it'd be a goner!"

The tall man nodded silently. "This was the last arrow Ben Slade had in his bow. It's a bad fire, but it won't do too much damage. When it burns itself out, he'll be all washed up."

Something ran out of the brush and loped across the clearing. Rip raised his gun before he saw it was only a coyote. The fire was burning so fiercely that even though the wind had begun to drop, the flames continued to leap ahead from one pile of brush to the next.

"Smoke's gittin' bad," the little one muttered. "We better drop back across the clearin'."

Rip was about to voice his agreement when a burst of shooting—five shots in all, closely spaced—swept his words away.

"That was across the wash, jest below the fill!" Grumpy rapped. "Cheng and the boys jumped somebody!"

The partners turned that way, riding at a gallop. Before they were fairly across the clearing, flames leaped up near the piled timbers. A swift-running pony caught their attention and they swung around, not knowing who the rider might be.

It was Cheng Bow, his yellow face tight with alarm. "That shooting—was it Moy and Lee? They were in close to the fill. I spoke to them only a few minutes ago."

Rip drove his knees into his bronc, calling back over his shoulder, "Come on! We'll find out what's happened!"

The new fire had gained headway rapidly. Flames were already licking at the timbers. In the lurid light, they could see nothing of Lee Kee and Moy.

"Give 'em a yell in Chinese!" Grumpy told Cheng.

The latter obliged with repeated calls but got no answer. McCandless and his foremen had routed out the crew and they were pouring into the wash, armed with shovels. No water being available, their only hope of saving even part of the timbers was by smothering the flames with earth. Heat and flying sparks drove them back repeatedly, lungs filled with smoke and hands and faces scorched.

The partners' foremost concern was to find Lee Kee and Moy Kim. It was impossible to get within a hundred feet of the spot where the second fire had started. Accompanied by Cheng, they got around behind the burning area. Cheng's shrill cries to the missing men again went unanswered. When the horses stubbornly refused to venture over the hot, smoking ashes and the smoldering skeletons of the fallen trees, Rip tried it on foot. Several such attempts convinced him that it couldn't be done.

"It's no use," he said reluctantly, as he backed out, slapping at the widening holes in his shirt where sparks had dropped. "It'll be an hour or two before we can go over the ground carefully. We won't know until then if they got caught in there."

"Depends on who was doin' that shootin'," the little one declared weightily. "They was mounted. If they didn't git cut down, they got out before the fire caught 'em. They may be miles away from here now, chasin' the skunks that lit this fire."

That possibility seemed unlikely to Rip. "I'd like to believe they were somewhere down the wash, but I can't. Five shots, close together, then no more. If there'd been a running fight, it wouldn't have sounded that way." He turned a sober face to Cheng Bow. "We won't give up hope that they're all right until we have to," he said feelingly. "I know Moy and Lee are your friends and countrymen. But you can appreciate how I feel. I got them into this job, and I've got to hold myself responsible for whatever has happened."

A cry from the trestle turned them that way. A locomotive had pushed a dump car, laden with earth, out on the finished section. The man who was doing the shouting was big Quan Jee. He wanted the engineer to push the car out a few feet farther. When it reached the very end of the rails the loose earth was sprayed over the exposed cribbing, the bottom tier of which was burning in several places. In the wash itself, half a hundred Chinese wielded their shovels tirelessly, braving the smoke and heat as they spread the dirt over the flaming planks and stanchions.

"Those yellow boys are doin' a good job!" Grumpy declared admiringly. "They'll save most of the cribbin'. The fire from above is burnin' out. Don't look as though it was goin' to jump the clearin'."

The dawn breeze acting as a back draft on the fire to the north, was checking its advance, and by the time the wind dropped to a gentle zephyr, any fear that the flames would leap across the clearing was removed.

To the south of the fill, McCandless personally was directing the fight to save the timbers. One pile was beyond saving, and he was satisfied to keep the fire from spreading. There, too, the worst of the conflagration was over. Dawn was coloring the sky before Rainbow got his attention.

"It ain't so bad, Rip," McCandless got out wearily as he wiped his grimy face. "Thanks to you, I don't mind saying. Your advice saved my hide this time."

"We can't count up the cost yet," the tall man said soberly. "We can't find hide nor hair of Lee Kee and Moy

Kim."

"No? My Chinese crew did themselves proud tonight. God knows what the effect on them will be if anything's happened to those two boys." The anxiety stamped on McCandless's face was proof enough of his concern. "What do you think happened?"

"I believe they were shot down and either killed or so badly wounded they couldn't get away before the fire got them."

"Good God, no!" McCandless groaned. "Whatever you do, Ripley, don't say anything to Quan Jee just yet; word will get around quick enough that the boys are missing." He shook his head gravely. "I as good as promised him that nothing would happen to Moy and Lee. And you—you assured Miss Seng you would look out for them. What about her? I know it would take only a word from her to pull every man off the job."

"You're asking me questions that I've been asking myself for the past hour," was Rainbow's tight-lipped answer. "It's getting light fast now. All we can do is wait until we can get in there and begin looking for them."

In the pitiless, unrelenting light of day, the wash presented a scene of blackened, smoking desolation. The fire was still burning in some places but no longer menacing the trestle and construction material. At camp, the cooks had breakfast ready and were ringing the bell. McCandless thanked the crew and sent the men out of the wash. He remained behind with the partners and Cheng Bow. Quan and the others were not aware that Lee and Moy were missing.

The ashes were cooling rapidly, and half an hour later Rip led the way over the ground where the fire below the trestle had originated. A cry from Cheng drew them his way. He had found two guns. The partners identified them as the rifles Lee and Moy had carried. Examination showed they had not been fired.

Spurred on by their find, the searching party spread out and covered an ever widening area until they were as much as a mile below the railroad clearing. They found no trace either of the missing men or their horses.

McCandless, the only one of the party who was unmounted, found himself lagging behind. Getting Rip's attention, he motioned him and the others to wait. The strain he had been under for the past several hours had left him exhausted.

"There doesn't seem to be any point in going farther," he said. "We know for certain those boys didn't get trapped in the fire; and that's about all we do know—aside from being sure that Slade is responsible for all this." He looked at Rainbow. "Do you think it possible he and his men carried the boys off?"

"You mean kidnaped them—to hold them as hostages?" The tall man's tone was incredulous.

"Well, yes—"

"Not a chance, Mac! Holding Lee and Moy wouldn't stop the work, and that's all Slade is out to do."

"Wait a second!" Grumpy interjected. "There's a couple of loose broncs wanderin' around over there. They're saddled. The gray looks like the one Moy rode. Stay here while I round 'em up."

The horses made no attempt to break away, and he was back with them in a few minutes.

"Their broncs, shore enough!" the little man called out, stating what was by now obvious to all. "No blood stains on either saddle!"

"Hair singed at all?" Rainbow asked.

"No—"

"That doesn't leave any room for speculation," Rip said, his face hard and flat. "We know Lee and Moy didn't use their guns. They were caught by surprise and killed. The horses bolted as the boys pitched to the ground."

"Well!" McCandless burst out, puzzled. "Seems to me you're leaving a lot of room for speculation. We found the guns, but no sign of Moy and—"

"They were carried off, Mac, but not the way you mentioned. They were dead."

"But why, Ripley? For what reason?"

"Because murder isn't murder unless you can produce

a corpus delicti. The bodies were carried off and buried somewhere."

"Buried where they will never be found!" came from Cheng Bow in quavering tones, his Oriental calm breaking. "It is not enough they were killed—but to be denied the right to sleep in the soil of their ancestors! You know what that means to us, Mr. Ripley!"

Rainbow placed a sympathetic hand on Cheng's shoulder. "I know, Cheng. I give you my word we'll find them; and we'll see that Slade and his blacklegs are brought to account for snuffing them out. You go ahead and build your railroad, Mac; we've got another job to do now."

"Don't shut me out of this, Rip," McCandless protested earnestly. "What can I do to help?"

"Send into town for the sheriff. Lockhart will play it our way this time, or we'll know why!"

CHAPTER TEN

IT WAS NOON before the sheriff arrived. He listened long and attentively to the partners and McCandless. He had little to say himself, and that little was guarded, if not evasive.

"You're trying awful hard to keep on the fence about this," Rainbow said accusingly, his patience worn out. "You know as well as we do that Ben Slade is responsible for what happened. Why don't you admit it, Lockhart? Who else but Slade could have done it?"

Lockhart shrugged noncommittally. "I dunno of anyone. But what I think ain't evidence. No one saw him in the wash. So far as we know, nobody ever heard him say he was goin' to burn you out."

"Forget about the fire for the present," Rip interrupted. "You've got evidence that Lee and Moy disappeared. Is there any question about that?"

Lockhart shook his head. "No argument about that. Considerin' the circumstances, I reckon they're dead. But I'm only guessin', same as you are. I can arrest Slade and his boys on suspicion. If I do, how long can I hold 'em? Without a charge, Slade's lawyer will have 'em out in forty-eight hours on a habeas corpus."

"Forty-eight hours—that may be enough," Rainbow said thinly. "Did you see any of them in town this morning?"

"No, but they coulda been there. The Gap's runnin' over with men these days."

"They been hangin' out at Mud Springs for a week or more," Grumpy interjected.

"So I understand," the sheriff responded, with a chilly glance.

"We won't ask you to go after them alone," said Rip. "My partner and I will ride with you." He was deliberately cutting across Lockhart's possible objections.

Cheng Bow had listened to every word in stony silence.

He did not speak now, but his eyes focused on Rainbow with an unvoiced appeal that the latter read without difficulty.

"All right, Cheng," the tall man told him, "you can go with us."

Lockhart started to object, only to grumble to himself. A few minutes later, they filed across the blackened wash and struck out for the hills to the west.

Lockhart was a sullen, hostile figure in the saddle. When he spoke at all it was only to growl some direction they were to take. His pretended disinterestedness went no deeper than his walrus hide. Under the surface, he was sorely troubled. Not that he expected Slade and his men to resist arrest; his concern was limited strictly to how much Ben might have to say if he found himself facing a murder charge. It was only a little matter of five hundred dollars, in Lockhart's case. At the time, it had loomed large. But it had gone the way easy money always goes. Looking back, he could only wonder why he had taken it.

After they crossed the road out of Mustang Gap, the partners recognized the trail they were taking as the one they had traveled on their previous trip to Mud Springs. Lockhart pulled up just before they went up the last ridge between them and the Springs. "I'll handle this job my own way," he said flatly. "If you fellas will keep yore mouths shut, I'll take 'em into custody without any gunplay. Understand?"

"Okay," Rip responded tersely. "But no slip-ups, Sheriff."

They reached the crest and looked down on the grassy flat around the Springs. Not only was there no one there, but no sign remained of the camp.

"Pulled out!" Grumpy growled in his disappointment.

"And not long ago," Rainbow observed. "Their fire is still smoldering. Let's go down."

They found the spot where the tarpaulin had been stretched. There the grass was matted down and worn thin. No other sign of the camp remained.

The tall man moved thoughtfully around the dying

fire. He caught Lockhart regarding him with an obscure interest. "What do you make of it, Sheriff?"

Lockhart was slow with his answer. "I dunno. They left things clean as a whistle—burned everythin'."

"Didn't they?" said Rip. He stuck his boot in the ashes and kicked out a burned fragment of cloth. "Burned the tarp and their blankets—even tossed their empty cans on the fire. Must have been quite a blaze, judging by the amount of ashes." He indicated the blackened end of a piece of aspen. "Looks like they broke up a dead tree or two. I wonder why?"

"If yo're askin' me, I can't tell you," Lockhart flared up. "Mebbe they figgered they wouldn't be needin' this stuff again."

"They could have left it," Rainbow pursued. "They were crowded for time, but they built this fire and stalled around until they were sure there was nothing left that anybody could salvage."

"They may have been tossin' stuff on the fire for a couple days," the sheriff argued contentiously, his narrow eyes mean and resentful. "You think you know all the answers. What makes you so damn shore this fire was lit this mornin'?"

"Because the wind blows just about as hard here as it does in the wash. If this fire had been burning for a day or two, the grass would be scorched farther back on one side than the other. But look at it—it's burned back evenly all around. This bonfire was set when there wasn't any wind at all. That would be any time after fivc o'clock this morning."

It answered Lockhart and he had no more to say.

"Reckon that's settled," Grumpy grunted. He was squatting on his toes, poking at the charred rubbish. When he looked up, he caught Rainbow's eye.

"Well?" the latter prompted.

"Rip, you thinkin' what I'm thinkin' about what's here?" The little man's tone was freighted with his own sober suspicion.

"I reckon I am," Rainbow said tightly. "We're going to

find out what's beneath these ashes. Cheng, you ride back to camp and get a couple shovels. Don't waste time talking with anybody. Get back here as quickly as you can."

After Cheng Bow left, Lockhart found an inviting place in the shade of the trees and stretched out on the grass to watch the partners puttering around the burned-out fire. Comfortable as his position was, his lanky body could not relax nor could he find any peace of mind. He was afraid their expectations would be realized when they started digging. If they found what they were looking for, the case against Slade would be airtight. *And when he finds he's up against it,* ran Lockhart's thoughts, *he'll turn on the judge and me and spill everythin' he knows!*

Once Slade was in jail, opportunities for closing his mouth forever, and quickly, would present themselves. Lockhart fell to considering them, desperate as they were. But he didn't have the stomach for such things. "What the hell!" he growled to himself. "Let him talk! I'm stringin' along with Ripley and the little fella!"

The partners' interest in the embers, along with Cheng Bow's hurried departure (obviously for the railroad camp), were easily comprehended by the eyes glued to a pair of binoculars on the ridge that formed the southern rim of the bowl around Mud Springs. When the watcher saw Rip and Grumpy break off aspen saplings and begin using them to sweep away the ashes, he waited no longer. Getting back to his horse, he hurried down the far side of the ridge and flashed away for Mustang Gap.

For all of Cheng's haste, the shadows were growing long by the time he got back to the Springs. The partners had the ashes and rubbish cleared away. With the first shovel full of earth, Rip turned up a clod of buried sod. Lockhart snatched at it and examined it briefly.

"Grass still green!" he rapped. "You had the right hunch, Ripley; this ground's been spaded up!"

They took turns digging. It did not take them long to find Lee Kee and Moy Kim lying in their shallow grave. Cheng backed away, covering his face with his hands. The sheriff got down on his knees and examined the bodies briefly. "It was gunfire that got 'em," he muttered gruffly. "They was dead when they was thrown in here."

He got to his feet, his cadaverous face sagging.

"That makes it murder, don't it?" Grumpy demanded.

"It's murder," Lockhart got out heavily, trying to pull himself together.

Rainbow only nodded and walked over to Cheng Bow. "My heart's as heavy as yours, Cheng," he said soberly. "We'll have to cover the grave so the coyotes don't get at them tonight. Tomorrow, we'll send the undertaker out. He'll prepare the bodies for shipment to California."

"Quan Jee will have to be informed," the young Chinese said, his voice unsteady. "He will know what to do."

"I want you to leave it to me to speak to Quan," Rip told him. "Grump and I will go to town with the sheriff and make sure that Slade and the other two are locked up. You better come along with us, Cheng."

Night closed down before they reached the Gap. O'Mara was doing so well with building the extension of the Lander division that there was finished roadbed for half a dozen miles north of town. Remarkable as it was, it did not interest the partners tonight. They pressed on to the Gap, and when they cantered up the main street, they glanced ahead to Slade's office. To their dismay, the place was dark.

"Where you going to start looking for them, Lockhart?" Rip inquired.

"The Idaho House. If they ain't there, I'll try the saloons, and Charley's Steak House; they eat there considerable."

The three men were not at the hotel nor in Charley's restaurant. Lockhart looked into half a dozen saloons without finding them. Gid Penny, the town marshal, came along the street. The sheriff asked him if he had seen Slade, Fanin, or Cleary.

"I saw 'em about three, four hours ago," Gid told him. "They must be around." Finding Lockhart in the company of the partners and Cheng Bow aroused his suspicions. "Somethin' up, Jim?"

"I want to git my hands on 'em," Lockhart answered and said no more.

"Suppose we go around to the hotel barn and ask Dobe if their broncs are there," Grumpy suggested.

The old barn boss shook his head when the question was put to him. "I ain't seen their hosses in days."

On the way back to the street, Lockhart said, "That don't necessarily mean they've pulled out."

"No," Rainbow agreed. "We'll have a look at Slade's office. If everything is in order up there, I'll be inclined to believe they're somewhere around town."

Crossing the street, he led the way up the stairs. The office door was not locked. He used his boot on it, stepping quickly aside as it swung inward. It went unchallenged.

"Nobody up here," Lockhart growled.

"And there won't be," said Rainbow, his voice rough and bitter with disappointment as he glimpsed the litter of torn papers on the floor. Even in the faint light reflected from the street, the signs of hurried flight were unmistakable. "We could turn this town upside down and we wouldn't find them. They've pulled out."

"But nobody coulda tipped them off, Rip," the little one demurred.

"That's right," Lockhart seconded, feeling himself under suspicion. "We ain't been out of each other's sight since noon." He turned on Cheng. "How about you?" he demanded surlily. "Did you see anybody when you went for the shovels?"

"Yes, but he was a mile away," the young Chinese answered nervously. "I—I don't believe he saw me."

"Wait!" Rip interrupted as Lockhart would have fired another question at Cheng Bow. "Let me handle this, Sheriff. Now you tell us in your own way exactly what happened, Cheng."

"I rode back to the road and turned north, Mr. Ripley. That was the way we came in. Just before I left the road for the wash, I glanced back. This man was riding toward town and moving very fast–"

"There you are!" Lockhart cried. "There's yore explanation! Slade had somebody watchin' the Springs. He saw enough to tell him the jig was up."

The partners could only agree with him.

Lockhart was familiar with the room. He found a lamp and lit it. "Looks like a snowstorm hit this place," he said with a heavy sigh as he lowered himself into a chair. He pulled at his mustache thoughtfully. "Catchin' up with 'em is goin' to be a helluva job!" For reasons of his own, he hoped they would never be apprehended. "They're either headin' for the Snake River towns or makin' tracks for Nevada. If you fellas think we could accomplish anythin', I'll organize a posse and we'll go out lookin' for 'em."

The tall man said no. "They made a clean getaway. With the start they've got, they won't be overhauled tonight."

"That's what I figger," Lockhart agreed, his tone, as much as his words, expressing the dim view he took of his chances. "There was no train out of the Gap since one o'clock; but they could be layin' up somewheres to catch the southbound local some place between here and Lander."

"Slade's too smart for that," Grumpy spoke up. "He knows you'll be telegraphin' the sheriff down there."

"That's right. I'll git off telegrams to a dozen Nevada officers. I'll wire the sheriffs along the Snake, too."

"It's worth a try," said Rip. "But I don't believe they'll go that way; it's too far. If they ride all night, they'll be in Nevada by morning, with two main-line railroads to get them out of the country in a hurry. By noon tomorrow, they can be in California, if that's their intention."

That made sense to Grumpy. "California could be the ticket. Slade knows his way around out there. The sheriff's got Miggles and Santell locked up. Mebbe we could git somethin' outa them. If it wa'n't no more'n where Slade hired 'em, it might give us a lead. Chances are he got hold of Cleary and Fanin at the same time."

"It's an idea," Lockhart conceded. "We can give it a try."

"They're all rolling stones," said Rainbow. "Where they

met up wouldn't tell us very much. But suppose the two of you give them a good grilling. If it's all right with you, Sheriff, Cheng and I will stay here and try to sort out some of these bits of paper. A man in as big a hurry as Slade was doesn't take time to tear up old letters unless he figures they contain information he doesn't want anyone to get his hands on."

"Help yourself," Lockhart told him. "You can see better if you light the big lamp. It'll be an hour or more before I git back; I'll have to see the district attorney and git my telegrams off."

"Take your time," Rip told him. "I'll have a long job here."

When they left, he lighted the hanging lamp and placed it on the floor. It didn't take him long to discover that, while matching the torn fragments of paper was not too difficult, certain pieces were missing. He found unmistakable evidence that they had been burned in the metal wastebasket.

When he had some of the jigsaw puzzles arranged, the words scrawled on them were easily read. Unfortunately, they were only harmless banalities about the weather and other trivia. The bottom half of the letter had been torn off. He took it for granted that it had been burned. When he carefully assembled another set of pieces, it proved to be nothing more interesting than a bill of sale for some horses.

Fitting the scraps of paper became a game, with Cheng Bow working as industriously as he. But their combined efforts failed to reward them with any pertinent information.

When they had been at it for the better part of an hour, Rip said, "We might as well give up, Cheng; Slade did a *thorough job of destroying the meat of these letters.* But he wasn't able to hide the fact that most of them were written by the same hand, though some are initialed N and some S."

"I noticed that, too, Mr. Ripley," the young Chinese observed studiously. "Am I correct in thinking that the writer's full initials are either S.N. or N.S.?"

"I'm sure that's the correct explanation." Rainbow selected some of the scraps and put them in his wallet. "Suppose we gather up the envelopes. Slade seems to have tossed them aside as though he didn't consider them of any interest. I'd like to check on the postmarks."

Some were marked *Portland—Seattle—Denver;* but fully a dozen were stamped *Buffalo Lodge, Montana*. He didn't attempt to conceal his elation.

"You find something of interest, eh?" Cheng queried, with an oblique smile.

"Very interesting, Cheng. Very interesting, indeed!"

Footsteps sounded on the stairs, and he hurriedly dropped a handful of the envelopes into his pocket. Cheng watched him carefully, his yellow face impassive.

"We won't mention this to the sheriff," Rip told him.

Cheng Bow nodded ever so slightly. "I have the greatest respect for your wisdom, Mr. Ripley."

Lockhart and Grumpy had Bemis Price with them. Being the county prosecutor, he was interested in the killing of Lee Kee and Moy Kim, but only in a professional sense. They were Chinese, hence of no importance. (That was the traditional Western viewpoint, dating back to the days of '49, and still held by many.) He examined the letters that Rip and Cheng had pieced together and agreed with the former that they contained nothing of value.

"I'll make a formal charge of murder against Slade, Fanin, and Cleary, in the morning," he announced. "I can't say I'm hopeful that we'll be able to pick them up. I believe you gentlemen know," he continued, addressing the partners, "that the county is not in a financial position to undertake an expensive search. Locally, we'll do all we can; but Lockhart says you are of the opinion that sending out a posse wouldn't accomplish anything."

"We are," Rainbow answered. "Slade didn't start running till he had to. He won't stop now until he's put a thousand miles between himself and Mustang Gap. Did Miggles and Santell have anything to say?"

"Not a thing," Grumpy answered. "Slade ain't been near

'em in days, but they refused to crack. Couldn't remember where he talked to 'em about comin' here. Miggles thought it was Butte; Santell figgered it was Seattle. They was lyin', of course."

"Naturally," Bemis said, with a very superior air. "I could have told you you wouldn't get anything out of them. It's lucky for them that they've been locked up for a couple weeks. Puts them in the clear on this double killing."

He stayed only a few minutes longer. Secretly, he was as well pleased as Lockhart—and for the same reason—that the partners were of the opinion that Slade and his pals had left the country for good. After he left, Rip asked the sheriff about an undertaker. Lockhart led them around the corner to Amos Baxter's establishment.

"I'll have to take a couple men with me," Baxter declared, when he learned what was wanted of him. "It's a long trip up to Mud Springs and back. It'll be expensive. Who foots the bill?" (He raised the question only because the dead men were Chinese.)

"Send your bill to Dan McCandless," Rainbow advised so sharply that a frightened look swept across the undertaker's pudgy face. "The railroad will arrange transportation to California."

When they stepped out on the street after concluding their business with Baxter, the sheriff announced that he was going home to supper.

"We better be thinking of getting something to eat ourselves," said Rainbow. On Cheng Bow's account, he decided against the Idaho House. Chinese, Indians, and Mexicans were not welcome there. "You take our horses around to the hotel barn," he told the young Chinese. "Tell the barn boss to give them a little grain. We'll be using them later tonight. We'll be waiting for you at Charley's Steak House."

By night, Mustang Gap was no longer just the boisterous little cow town it had been less than two weeks ago. In twos and threes, and groups of a dozen or more, the men from O'Mara's camp thronged the street. Stores that had formerly closed at six now stayed open, prospering on the Denver and Pacific payroll. As for the saloons, they were reaping a harvest, as the judge had predicted.

Grumpy observed the scene with a jaundiced eye, and as soon as he and Rip were alone, he said, "The town's bulgin' at the seams, but the broncs was all right where they was—or was you jest gittin' rid of Cheng for a minute?"

"That was the idea," the tall man confessed. "I've something to tell you. I believe I've located the party who has been putting up the money for Slade."

"Yeh?" the little one muttered, trying not to look surprised. "Where?"

"Buffalo Lodge, Montana. Do you know the town?"

"No. It must be a small place. What's the party's name?"

"I don't know. His initials are either N.S. or S.N. Let's get out of this mob, and I'll explain. Here—this doorway will do."

The facts concerning the envelopes and the initialed letters were quickly told. To Rainbow's surprise, Grumpy agreed heartily with the conclusions he had reached. "But I don't see the importance of it—comin' now, Rip. The hoss is gone, so why bother lockin' the barn? You shore ain't figgerin' that Slade is headin' for this town in Montana?"

"Maybe I am at that. It's certainly possible. When a man's in trouble, he hunts up his friends."

"Not when he's jest lost a big wad of money for 'em," the little man dissented caustically.

"You've hit the nail on the head without realizing it," Rainbow argued. "It's just because Slade dropped a lot of money that I'm so positive he'll be getting in touch with this party in Buffalo Lodge. Nobody but a crook would go into a get-rich-quick scheme with Ben Slade. You don't run out on that kind, Grump; you try to square yourself. I believe if we can locate this character in Montana, and watch him without tipping our hand, he'll lead us to Slade, sooner or later."

"By Joe, when I look at it from that angle, it makes sense," Grumpy declared thoughtfully. "We've played longer shots than that and made them stand up. Is it yore idea for us to pull out for Montana?"

"Not right away. Before we leave for camp tonight, I'm going to wire Mei-lang and ask her to meet us here in the Gap as soon as she can arrange it. I want to talk this whole thing over with her. I want her to understand that we're going to stay with this case until we grab the men who killed Moy and Lee. And it will be at our own expense."

"Of course!" the little one agreed promptly. "But can't you write her all that?"

"No, I want to talk to her, Grump. I'm going to ask her to help us. We don't know Buffalo Lodge, but there may be someone there who knows us. It would be foolish to make the long trip to Montana and barge into that town without having some advance information. Mei-lang can get it for us if anyone can."

"I dunno," Grumpy muttered, with a disapproving toss of his head. "When she hears how Moy and Lee was murdered, she'll be anxious to do anythin' she can to help us track down the killers. But you better think it over, Rip; you could be sendin' her off on a mighty dangerous job."

"I've thought of that," Rainbow replied, his mouth tightening. "We'll go with her as far as Billings. When she's ready, she can get in touch with us. I never saw a Montana town that didn't have a Chinese quarter. We've seen her slip into the Chinatowns of Nevada without white men ever knowing she was there. There's no reason to believe she can't do it in Buffalo Lodge. If things go wrong and she gets into trouble, it won't be the first time the three of us have faced it together. Let's go into the restaurant. Cheng will be along in a minute."

CHAPTER ELEVEN

BILLINGS HAD CHANGED since the partners had seen it last; it was bigger, noisier, and more prosperous. There were other changes, and they were not to Grumpy's liking.

"She's losin' her Western flavor," he complained disgustedly. "Look at that sign on the window. 'Coffee Shoppey'! And across the street—'Beauty Saloon'! 'Paris Bootery'! This used to be a he-man's town. Paris Bootery!" he snorted contemptuously. "Twenty years ago, even ten, the gent who owns that place wouldn't have dared put up such a sign. If he had, some right-minded cowpuncher woulda heaved a rock through the window!"

"If it gripes you as much as that, you better write a letter to the chamber of commerce," Rainbow advised facetiously. "There's nothing I can do about it." In quite another tone, he added, "I've got other things on my mind. We've been waiting here five days now to hear from Meilang. If I don't get some word from her by tomorrow, we're heading for Buffalo Lodge."

"That would be a smart move!" the little one observed sarcastically. "There's no reason to believe anythin' has gone wrong. You sent her down there to git some information. It's jest takin' her longer than we figgered."

Rip was not impressed with such logic. "Maybe it was a mistake to send Cheng Bow with her," he said. "He's pretty young and not too experienced."

"He'll look out for her," Grumpy insisted. "Cheng's all right. But we didn't send him down there jest to act as her bodyguard; he knows the men we're after and would recognize 'em on sight; Mei-lang wouldn't know 'em from Adam. Back in the Gap, that was yore argument for bringin' him along."

"That's true," the tall man acknowledged, "but what I said a moment ago still stands; we'll wait another day, and no longer. Let's walk back to the hotel. A letter may have arrived."

He found a letter waiting for him, but it was from Dan McCandless. Dan wrote that things were going so well that he expected to be across the wash with the cribbing completed by the end of the week. (Before leaving southern Idaho, Rip had driven Mei-lang out to the camp again, where she had conferred with McCandless and Quan Jee. Her assurances to the latter that she and the partners, with the full support of the company, were determined to track down the men who had killed Lee Kee and Moy Kim had satisfied the big man.) The manner in which the work was progressing was proof enough of how the Chinese crew had responded. *I'll appreciate it if you'll write me as soon as you have something encouraging to report that I can pass on to Quan Jee,* the letter concluded. *I have suggested to MacDonald that we name the new junction Rainbow, in your honor.*

"Rainbow, Idaho, eh?" Grumpy chuckled. "Sounds all right. You better not write Mac that we're still sittin' here, twiddlin' our thumbs, or he might change his mind about honorin' you."

"There may be something to that," Rip said, managing a smile. "With things going so well with him, I reckon McCandless is seeing some *real* rainbows, at last. I wish we could see one."

He received a message from Mei-lang the following morning, and it came not from Buffalo Lodge but from the house of Lum Far, the wealthy proprietor of the Crystal Café, in Billings. It was there that she and Cheng Bow had prepared themselves for the visit to Buffalo Lodge. Dressed in cheap, ill-fitting attire, and carrying the inevitable scuffed paper suitcase, they had emerged to masquerade as humble John Chinaman and his wife, bound somewhere to open a laundry or the like.

This morning, when the partners were shown in, she was her poised, beautiful self again.

Lum Far excused himself at once.

"Perhaps you would prefer that I leave, too, Mr. Ripley," Cheng suggested.

"That isn't necessary," said Rainbow, his attention fixed anxiously on Mei-lang. "You were gone much longer than you expected. Did you run into trouble?"

"No, everything went as planned." She smiled at him fondly. "I might have known you would be worried, not hearing from me. I wanted to write, but I thought it best not to address a letter to you. Letters have strange ways of being seen by the wrong people—haven't they?"

"If that wasn't so, we wouldn't be in Billings," Grumpy declared, with a little chuckle. "I told Rip you could take care of yoreself."

Ignoring the interruption, Rainbow said, "Were you able to locate our man, Mei-lang?"

"Very easily. His name is Noah Swayne."

"Noah Swayne—" Rainbow caught the little one's eye. "Do we know him, Grumpy?"

The latter ran back through the pages of his memory and said, "He's a new one. What's his business, Mei-lang?"

"Promotions. His ventures have a habit of ending disastrously for the people who put money into them." She noted Rip's puzzled look, and smiled. "I see you are asking yourself where I got my information regarding Mr. Swayne. I shouldn't have to remind you that no one pays any attention to Chinese waiters, cooks—migratory workers. But my countrymen have eyes and ears; they see and hear many things. They may be in Seattle or Butte this year and in Buffalo Lodge the next. This man Swayne has been there about ten months. He has taken over a two-story brick building on the main street of the town and unquestionably has strong backing; and not just locally. His financial and political connections are wider than that."

"So far, the shoe fits," Rip observed. "Swayne could use a man with Ben Slade's talents. What about Slade and the other two? Were you able to get a line on them?"

"They're not there now. Cheng thinks Slade may have been in Buffalo Lodge a day or two before we arrived."

"I'll explain why I think so, Mr. Ripley," Cheng volunteered. "An aged Chinese, Hong Chew, is employed as janitor by Swayne. He is there all day and sometimes in the evening. From him I learned that Swayne had a visitor, a stranger to Hong Chew. It was in the evening, and they had a violent argument. I asked the old man to describe this visitor. The description he gave me fits Slade."

"What happened after that—after the quarrel, I mean?" Rip asked, with quickened interest. "Was that the last the old man saw of this stranger?"

"No, Hong Chew saw him again the following morning. It was early. When Hong came to work, he found this stranger and several others waiting downstairs in front of Swayne's place. Huggins came out of the office and they rode off together. Slade—if it was Slade—has not been seen since."

"Who is Huggins?"

"He's Noah Swayne's right-hand man," Mei-lang answered. "Cheng feels that since Swayne's visitor left Buffalo Lodge on horseback he has not quit the country. I agree with him. We know Swayne has a number of men, maybe as many as a dozen, thugs and gunmen, operating from some secret hide-out in the Medicine River Range. I feel sure that the man who left town with Huggins went up to join them."

"Wait a minute," Grumpy protested. "This is gittin' confused. Let's go back to the beginnin'. Swayne's in a fight, I gather. What's it all about, and what's his game?"

"I'm sorry," Mei-lang murmured, with an apologetic smile. "I have so much to tell you that I hardly know how best to begin. I secured a map in Buffalo Lodge and marked it so it would be easier for you to understand what I have to say. Suppose we have a look at it."

Cheng cleared a table and spread out the map. Mei-lang found a pencil.

"Here," she said, indicating a point on the map, "is Buffalo Lodge. It's a small city of eight, perhaps nine thousand people. And here, some forty miles to the south, is the little town of Nazareth. Its only connection with the outside world is by daily stage to Buffalo Lodge. To go back a bit, you can see a county line running across here, from east to west before it dips sharply south and strikes into the mountains." Mei-lang glanced up at Rainbow. "I think that is something to keep in mind."

"You mean it puts Buffalo Lodge in one county and Nazareth in another?" Rip queried.

"Exactly. It gives Nazareth its own officials, and Noah Swayne has no friends among them. But to go on with our geography. You can see how the Medicine River Range forms a half-circle on the south and west of this big basin—Nazareth Basin it is called—and over here on its eastern limits is Medicine River. It's all cow country; ranches all over the basin and on the benchlands to the south and west. It's so rich, beautiful, that it is easy to understand why the people who live there love it so."

Rainbow frowned as he caught her enthusiasm. "You don't sound as though you were just reporting what someone had told you," he observed.

"No," she admitted readily. "Cheng and I spent two days in Nazareth. I knew the basin and all that high country—it's a long uphill climb from Buffalo Lodge—was aflame with violence. I thought I knew why. But it was based on hearsay, so I decided to get the truth for myself—The two of you needn't shake your heads; Cheng and I were perfectly safe."

"You still haven't told us what this is all about," Grumpy grumbled impatiently. "I take it this gent Swayne is out to grab somethin' and is puttin' the heat on those folks in Nazareth Basin. But what does he want? What's he after?"

"Medicine River, Grumpy. Not part of it; he wants it all. It's a fast-flowing mountain stream. When it goes on a rampage, parts of Buffalo Lodge are put under water. The town has had several serious floods. For years it has been calling for flood control. Swayne took advantage of that and got a bill through the legislature authorizing him to turn Medicine River into Nazareth Basin and build a dam to hold back the water he impounds. When he has acquired seventy-five per cent of the land needed for the project, the state will condemn the rest and the owners will be forced to sell at a fair appraisal of the property's value." Mei-lang's glance traveled from Rainbow to the little man. "I don't believe it's necessary to tell you that flood control plays a very minor part in Swayne's plans."

"Indeed you don't," said Rip. "Water power—that's what he's after. It's an old story with us, Mei-lang. We've seen that game played many times. My sympathies are all with those folks in the basin. They'll be mighty lucky if they don't lose their homes and get pushed out. Politicians never think of such things, if they see a way to line their pockets. But it isn't our fight. We didn't come all the way from Mustang Gap to get tangled up in that sort of a scrap. It's Slade we're after."

The little one nodded in silent agreement, only to have Mei-lang say, "I'm afraid we can't keep out of it. In fact, I believe the sooner we get into it the better. As you would expect, Swayne had things his own way at first, sending his gunmen into the basin to snipe at cattle, fire haystacks, and burn down several ranch houses. People who could be intimidated fell into line and sold out to him. He's still pursuing those tactics, but he's not making any headway; resistance in the basin is organized now; it would be as much as a man's life is worth to turn traitor and sell even an acre of rangeland to Swayne."

She wasn't finished, but she paused to find the partners regarding her closely, obviously unmoved by what she had said.

"My point is this," she continued, ignoring their unvoiced objections. "When a man of Swayne's caliber gets so deeply involved in a proposition that he can't pull out—and finds it going against him—he invariably does one thing; he brings in reinforcements and throws caution to the winds. Swayne is in exactly that position right now. A stalemate won't help him; it's got to be win or lose all with him. I think it is reasonable to believe that if Slade and the other two men we want are not already on hand that it will be only a matter of days before they come. Slade is in Swayne's debt. To use your own words, he'll go all out to square his account. How better can he do it than by getting into this water fight?"

"By grab, she's right!" Grumpy exclaimed, in a sudden about-face. "Nazareth Basin is the honey pot that will draw in the flies for us, Rip!"

Mei-lang gave him a grateful smile. "You put it better than I can, Grumpy. We can make sure we'll catch the flies we're interested in if we join the cause of the Nazareth men and make it our cause. What do you have to say, Rainbow?"

The tall man got to his feet and walked the length of the room and back, his lean face sober and thoughtful. At last, he said in his quiet way, "You make it sound very simple, Mei-lang. I assure you it wouldn't be that simple. I think there's good reason to believe that Slade, and possibly Pete Cleary and Joe Fanin, will appear in the basin sooner or later. I'm not at all convinced, however, that we can help ourselves by getting into this fight. At this distance, I don't know how we could help the basin men. But this I'm sure of—Grumpy and I would have to work under cover; once Slade learned that we were in Nazareth, he'd know why we were there."

"And you figger he'd run, eh?" the little one interjected.

"It would depend on the circumstances. If I understand Ben Slade, he'd size up the backing he'd have and if it looked good enough to him, he'd have a try or two at rubbing us out before he decided it was time to run."

"And that worries you?" Grumpy demanded crustily.

"Not at all. If I thought we could keep our identity secret for a week or two, I'd take a chance on this proposition. I know we could work our way into the basin without tipping our hand. But a couple peddlers or tinkers, drifting through that country at a time like this, would be under suspicion as soon as they showed their faces. We'd have to take some influential man into our confidence."

"That is undoubtedly true," Mei-lang said at once. "Matthew Cameron is the man for you to contact. His ranch is located at the head of the basin. He's not only a well-to-do stockman but he represents the Nazareth district in the legislature. I learned that when Swayne had his flood-control bill introduced, Mr. Cameron fought tooth and nail to defeat it. I know he is highly regarded by his neighbors; and though no one will come out and say so, I believe he is the leader of the basin men."

Grumpy nodded to himself. "Sounds like a man who'd respect a confidence."

"That's the reputation he bears," said Mei-lang. Her voice had a calm, dispassionate quality as it carried across the room to Rainbow, who stood at the window, his back to her, absent-mindedly gazing at the street below. "Co-operating with him would mean that we could be sure of getting help if we needed it."

Rip faced her suddenly, his eyes stern, troubled. "You use the word 'we,' Mei-lang. Somehow, you give me the feeling that you are not referring just to Grump and me. By any chance are you including yourself?"

"I am," she answered simply. "Cheng and I are returning to Nazareth tomorrow." Her lips had lost their alluring curve and her mouth was firm and resolute. "There are several Chinese families living there. One of them, Johnny Wong and his wife—Johnny Wong is American for Wong Shon—conduct a small restaurant. We will live with them; it's all arranged. Cheng will pass himself off as a new man in the kitchen; I will go against custom and be in front, acting as cashier. The restaurant is only three doors from the post office. It's well patronized. I'm sure if I keep my eyes and ears open I will be able to pick up some information for you that you might not be able to get any other way."

Rainbow just stood there shaking his head for a moment or two. "It will be dangerous; and you know it," he said at last. "You'll be there as a spy; if you're found out, there's no telling what may happen to you." He turned to Grumpy for support. "We can't permit her to take a chance like that."

"Wal, I dunno." The little one pursed his lips and gave Mei-lang a sly, approving glance. "This young woman has got her mind made up, Rip, and I reckon she ain't goin' to be talked out of it. And I don't see why you should try;

she knows how to play her cards. We could drop into that restaurant from time to time and keep an eye on her. When she has some news to pass on to us, it can be done without anybody bein' the wiser."

Rip left the window and came back to his chair at the table, frankly perplexed. In his preoccupation, his thoughts were so close to the surface that Mei-lang read them without difficulty.

"Please, Rainbow, don't deny me the right to do what I can to help you." She placed her hand on his and searched his face with her dark, sober eyes. "I know you are thinking only of my safety. Believe me, I would do far more than just returning to Nazareth if I thought it would lead to the capture of the men who murdered Lee Kee and Moy. It isn't only that the two were murdered; it was the manner in which their bodies were desecrated that I can't forgive. I'll never be satisfied until Slade and his companions are taken back to Idaho and made to pay for what they did."

Never before had she spoken about the killing of Lee and Moy with such deep feeling. Rip studied her soberly, his lips lightly parted. The seconds ticked away before he said, "All right, if it means that much to you. Return to Nazareth as soon as it's convenient. It will be four or five days before we get there. When we meet in Johnny Wong's restaurant, make it appear that we are strangers. We'll drop in frequently and let you know where we can be reached. You'll have Cheng with you. If an emergency arises, it'll be up to him to get in touch with us in a hurry."

"You can depend on me, Mr. Ripley," the young Chinese declared with Oriental gravity. He bowed to Mei-lang. "I won't fail you."

With all the regal dignity of a queen acknowledging the loyalty of a devoted follower, she said, "I'm sure you won't, Cheng Bow." She turned and her eyes came to rest on Rip. She had won his consent, but she sensed it was with reservations. "What is it, Rainbow? Do you really want to go ahead with our plans?"

"I think it would be foolish not to go ahead. But," he

continued, "let's face up to the fact that all this may be for nothing. Slade may not be within a thousand miles of Nazareth Basin."

"I realize that. We're only playing a hunch—as you and Grumpy put it."

The tall man nodded. "Keep that in mind, Mei-lang. If we fail, it won't hurt so much."

CHAPTER TWELVE

THE SQUEAKING, SWAYING VEHICLE that toiled slowly over the uphill road to Nazareth this morning was a peddler's wagon of ancient vintage, its homemade wooden top warped and sun-cracked, its canvas side curtains dingy and frayed. It could be entered at the rear by means of a wooden step suspended on iron brackets. Inside, there was an arrangement of drawers and bins, filled with odds and ends of dry goods, notions, men's furnishings (overalls, work gloves, and the like) and cheap jewelry. Scabious patches of peeling paint of various colors were like the hashmarks on a veteran's sleeve, giving proof of its long service and many owners.

The two decrepit, bony horses that drew the wagon were in perfect harmony with the rest of the outfit, their halting, uncertain gait speaking eloquently of stiffening joints and hardening arteries, as were the two shabby, unshaven men who sat hunched over on the spring seat. Contrary to appearances, they were new to this business, having purchased the outfit only a week back, in faraway Billings. Avoiding Buffalo Lodge, they had turned south and reached the Nazareth road early the preceding day.

A pint-sized individual held the reins, and though he and his companion were in a hurry, he turned in at every cabin and ranch house they found. It fell to the tall, stringy-looking man seated beside him to announce their coming by beating on an iron frying-pan suspended from the roof, the pan serving in lieu of a bell. It was an almost unnecessary proceeding, since their coming was usually noted well in advance of their arrival.

Needless to say, the two men were Rainbow and Grumpy. Since reaching the Nazareth road, they had found themselves out of luck as far as business was concerned; but they were more interested in conversation than business. By arrangement, Grumpy did most of the talking. He had the knack of coloring his speech with backwoods vernacular and being garrulous and convincingly guileless.

"Ain't nothin' along here but scenery," the little man remarked when they failed to find a human habitation in the course of several miles.

To the right of the road, a scraggly forest of white pine marched up the hills to the crest of the Medicine River Range.

"Sawmill in there somewhere," said Rip. "I hear the saw whining."

Around the next bend, they got a glimpse of the mill. Half a dozen men were in evidence. Grumpy turned in, and Rainbow started banging the frying-pan. It brought an aproned man to the door of the cookshack. He had a tremendous paunch and a drooping, pear-shaped face. "When yuh turned in, I thought yuh was old Caleb," he said, wiping his flour-stained hands on his apron. "That's his wagon."

"It is," Grumpy agreed. "We bought Caleb out, team, wagon, and everythin'. Be yuh needin' anythin' this mornin'? We got a special bargain on some nice socks. Two bits a pair."

The cook nodded. "I can use a couple pair. Might blow myself to a pair of suspenders, too."

Grumpy got down, and while he was inside the wagon, several men came over from the mill and made some trifling purchases.

"Don't see many folks on the road," the little one observed as he made change.

"No, they're stayin' to home," the cook told him. "Trouble up in the basin. That where yo're headin'?"

"Yep—"

"Range trouble?" Rainbow queried without interest.

"Of a sort. The way I git it, there's a party in the Lodge who's buyin' up everythin' he can git his hands on and doin' his damnedest to drive the folks out who won't sell. Goin' to build a dam and make a big lake outa the basin. That's to keep the towns down below from bein' flooded when the river goes crazy. We figgered we'd strike him for a job when we got done sawin'; but he's run into a snag. Them folks around Nazareth say they ain't goin' to be run out."

"Yuh reckon they mean it?" Grumpy pretended to be more interested in knotting the leather thong on his change pouch than in the cook's answer.

"I dunno," the latter declared, pursing his lips. "Somebody's been makin' things tough for this fella—Swayne his name is—burnin' his houses and tarrin' and featherin' his agents. Mebbe it's jest kids. We had a Nazareth boy workin' here. When he heard what was goin' on up above, he asked for his time and told me he was goin' home to take a hand in the fight. Reckon both sides are sizin' up all strangers. But the two of yuh won't have no trouble; nobody's goin' to bother a couple peddlers."

"No reason why they should," Grumpy said lightly. "We're here today and gone tomorrow."

He got the team moving and the wagon was soon back on the road.

"It helps some when they recognize this outfit," Rip commented. "Maybe we should make it a point to have something to say about old Caleb every time we stop."

"Right," the little one grunted. "Do you figger that cook knows what he's talkin' about, sayin' kids are mixed up in this fight?"

"By kids, he meant boys of eighteen to twenty-one or so. If they're runnin' wild, they'll do the basin folks more harm than good. Boys of that age always get over their heads, Grump. You know how it was in the Squaw Valley war."

During the course of the day they made numerous stops, sold a little merchandise, and garnered some useful bits of information. Though their performance as a couple of itinerant peddlers was so convincing that no one questioned that they were other than what they pretended to be, they were strangers, possibly Swayne agents, and on that score they could not escape suspicion. Grumpy had called on his imagination and concocted the story that old Caleb had gone to California to escape the cold Montana winters. He supplied all the details, though he hadn't the slightest idea of the man's whereabouts.

At the gait at which the old team moved Nazareth was still a day's journey ahead of them. With that in mind, they made camp early enough to give their fire time to burn out before darkness fell. Medicine River and the road ran within a hundred yards of each other for several miles along here. Turning off across a sage-dotted flat, they reached the cottonwoods and willows that lined the bank.

After supper, with dishes dried and stowed away for the night, Rip said, "We have no reason to believe we're being watched, but we'll be on the safe side and move the wagon up the river a few yards when it gets dark. If anybody is planning to throw a shot at us tonight, we won't be here to stop it."

The little one nodded phlegmatically. "And it might not be a bad idea to git our rifles out of the wagon after we spread our blankets." He filled his pipe as he sat on the ground, his back propped comfortably against a log, and put a match to the bowl. Presently the pleasant aroma of strong tobacco was mingling with the smoke of the dying fire. "This is a right nice spot for a night camp," he mused, listening to the rushing river. "That kinda music should put a man to sleep in a hurry."

"You turn in early," said Rip. "I'll try to keep an eye open till midnight. It's going to be black in here until the moon gets high."

In the deepening twilight his voice had a plaintive, troubled note. Grumpy gave him a slow, searching glance.

"What's botherin' you, Rip?"

"Just thinking about Mei-lang. We're two or three days behind schedule. By now, she must be wondering what's become of us."

"She won't do nothin' foolish; that girl's got a level head. Anyways, we'll be seein' her tomorrow evenin'."

When night fell, they moved the wagon a few yards and picketed the horses. Grumpy spread his blankets and was soon sound asleep.

The air was still, not a leaf stirring, but the growling

river drowned out the lesser night sounds. Something moved out on the flat. The careful steps were only a few feet away when Rainbow caught them. He reached for his gun and waited. The intruder proved to be only a deer, coming down to drink. The frightened animal caught his scent a moment later and bounded away in panic.

Even the growling of the river could not blot out the distant yipping of the coyotes. Otherwise, the night remained peaceful. When it got to be ten o'clock, and moonlight began to creep down the foothills opposite, Rainbow decided he could turn in without awakening Grumpy; but as he was pulling off his boots, he caught the swift running of ponies moving over the road from the direction of the basin.

Two horses—coming downhill, and coming fast, he said to himself. He got to his feet and cocked his ear. The tattoo of thudding hoofs was rapidly moving nearer. "This may be company," he muttered grimly.

He got his rifle from beneath the blanket. Tension built up in him as he waited. In the moonlight, he saw two riders swing into view. They were raking their mounts with the spurs. They came on and on, and for a moment he thought they were cutting across the flat to the wagon. But they were only clipping off a curve in the road. A few seconds later they drove past and were gone without slackening their mad pace.

"Those gents is in an awful hurry, Rip!"

The tall man swung around to find Grumpy sitting up in his blankets.

"None of our business," Rip said. "I caught 'em glancing back once or twice as though they were concerned with what was behind them. Listen!"

Down the road from Nazareth Basin came another beating of hoofs. Not two riders this time, but ten or more.

"Reckon this explains why those gents who jest passed was high-tailin' it hell-bent for election," the little one growled, reaching for a gun.

"Sit tight," Rainbow jerked out tensely. "Time enough for us to mix into this when we know it concerns us."

Conversation stopped with that. Stiffly alert, their eye glued on the road, the partners saw the pursuing riders shadowy figures in the moonlight, swing around the bend. In a few moments the horsemen, a dozen strong, raced past leaving the air heavy with the dust of their riding. Not moving, Rainbow and the little man waited until the drumming of hoofs was drowned out by the grumbling river. Grumpy pulled on his boots and he and Rip walked out on the flat a few feet to get away from the river's noises.

They were in time to catch a series of spattering shots a mile or more away. Those first shots were hotly answered. When the thunder of gunfire died away in the foothills the night was still again.

"That was hot and heavy while it lasted," was Rip's tight-lipped comment. "Some of those slugs must have found their mark."

He found Grumpy staring at him owlishly. "You've always got an answer. What do you make of it?"

Rainbow shrugged thoughtfully. "If a guess will do you, I'll give you one. That big bunch were basin men. I figure they smoked out a couple of Swayne's agents and either killed them or ran them out of the country."

The little man's eyes narrowed in his hard-bitten face. "Reckon that's it. Gives us a purty good idea of what we're gittin' into. These basin folks ain't foolin'— That bunch will be comin' back directly."

"In a few minutes," Rip agreed. "Suppose we go out a little farther and lie in the sage; I want to have a look at that crowd. It won't surprise me if they're coming back with an empty saddle or two."

"By grab, you don't know yore own mind tonight," Grumpy protested irascibly. "Thought we wasn't mixin' in this. Now you want to go out on the flat. If that bunch spots us, we'll be lucky if we don't git the same treatment they gave that other pair."

"That's right," Rainbow conceded. "It's taking a chance, but it's worth it."

Concealing their rifles in the trees, they got their hand

guns out of the wagon and started across the flat. Thirty feet from the road they flattened out in the shadow of a clump of sagebrush. They hadn't been there long when they heard the basin men returning, their broncs held to a walk. It seemed to confirm the tall man's surmise that the party had suffered some casualties.

Presently, the partners could hear the men talking, though it was not possible to catch what they were saying. They came on, and when they passed, two of them were supporting a third man between them. Another kept his saddle only by clutching his saddle horn.

"Looks like that sawmill cook knew what he was talkin' about," Grumpy muttered as Rip and he made their way back to the wagon. "Jest kids; not a one of them over twenty, twenty-one! They ain't dry behind the ears yet. If that's all Swayne's got to worry about, he won't have to throw Ben Slade and his pals into the scrap."

"You know better than that," Rip said sharply. "Chances are those boys are acting on their own. Their folks may not know anything about it."

"They'll know tomorrow, by gravy! Two of those boys are hurt bad. That means a doctor." Grumpy scowled as his thoughts ran ahead to the next day. "You can bet yore tintype we ain't heard the last of this. When we show up in the mornin' there won't be no denyin' that we camped along the river tonight. We're goin' to be asked a lot of questions. What did we see? What did we hear?" Without giving Rainbow an opportunity to answer, he added, "We better git our story straight right now. What's it goin' to be?"

"We'll have to stick to the truth, Grump; not the whole truth, but a reasonable facsimile. It would be foolish to deny we spent the night here. We heard men on the road, and the shooting. We didn't know what it meant, and we didn't figure it was any of our business."

They made an early start the next morning. In the course of several miles, the country opened up ahead of them and they knew they were in Nazareth Basin. Rainbow found it as pleasing as Mei-lang had described it. Grumpy was equally impressed.

"Water, buffalo grass, mountains to shelter it against winter storms—it's got everythin' a cowman could want! A man who'd even think of drownedin' it out ought to be boiled in oil."

Rip's answer was restricted to a laconic "Yeh." He was thinking about Mei-lang. She had never been out of his thoughts for long since they parted in Billings. Though he knew her shrewdness and wisdom had never failed her in a dangerous situation, he could not help wondering, and with unashamed anxiety, how she had fared in Nazareth.

"You'll see her this evenin'," the little one said, with a chuckle. "I bet Johnny Wong's restaurant is doin' some business these days, with her behind the desk. Wouldn't surprise me if all the cowpokes around Nazareth are droppin' in whether they're hungry or not— Here's a house! Start bangin' the fryin'-pan!"

CHAPTER THIRTEEN

THE NOISY SUMMONS brought a bearded six-footer to the door. He recognized the wagon at once and started to fling up a hand in friendly greeting. A quick change took place in his attitude when he saw that it was not old Caleb on the seat. "Turn around and drive on!" he ordered with a sharp edge of hostility. "We don't need nuthin'!"

"Okay!" Grumpy answered obligingly, but as he clucked to the horses, a gaunt-looking woman, her scraggly hair tied in a knot on the top of her head, popped out of the kitchen.

"Pa, I need some calico!" she protested shrilly. "I bin promisin' Effie a new dress fer months. Let me see what these fellers has."

Her husband glared his annoyance but let her have her way. She stepped into the wagon with Grumpy, while he kept his position at the door, regarding Rainbow with sullen suspicion. "Whar yuh from?" he asked when Grumpy reappeared.

"Billings—" the little man informed him and got no further.

"I mean whar yuh from this mornin'? Whar did yuh put up last night?"

"Down the river a couple miles," came from Grumpy. He knew where this was leading and he faced up to it with guileless innocence. "We heard some shootin' about an hour or so before midnight. Didn't know what it meant, but we figgered it wa'n't none of our business. I allus say the less yuh know about what don't consarn yuh, the better off yuh are. Here's yore change, ma'am. I hope yo're here when we come through ag'in next spring."

The bearded man snapped erect. "What do yuh mean by that?" Under his shaggy brows his eyes were grim.

"Why—the cook downriver at the sawmill told us some big highbinder was buyin' up everythin' around here. Goin' to build a dam and put Nazareth Basin under water." Grumpy shook his head regretfully. "What a shame that'd be! It ain't up to me to advise yuh what to do, but I'd think twicest before I sold out. I've seen a lot of country in my time, but yuh won't find better range than this anywheres."

"There won't be no more sellin' out to Noah Swayne," the bearded rancher responded grimly. "Any double-crossin' skunk that tries it better git ready fer his funeral. If we have to spill our blood to keep what's ourn, we'll do it."

"Yo're right," Grumpy agreed, climbing over the wheel to the seat. "When one of these here pirates moves in on yuh, yuh gotta stick together or yo're licked. But gittin' men to stick together ain't easy; there allus seems to be somebody ready to turn rat if he gits his price; and usually it's someone yuh least suspect."

"Humph!" the woman snorted triumphantly. "Pa, that's jest what I bin sayin' since I got back from Nazareth! Buyin' store clothes, she was; goin' off to visit her folks in Spokane! Where's the money comin' from, I'd like to know? Some folks has peculiar ways of gittin' it, I say!"

"Lucy, yo're lettin' yore tongue git awful loose!" her husband admonished angrily. The woman was not to be silenced that easily.

With a defiant toss of her head, she whipped out sarcastically, "Pity yuh can't git yore eyes open! Takes a woman to smell a rat; menfolks is too trustin'. Even Matt Cameron don't know what his own son is doin'."

She slammed into the kitchen before he could order her inside. "Don't pay no attention to her babblin'," he told the partners. "If she ain't workin' her jaw, she ain't happy."

The wagon rolled away.

"Too bad he shut her up," Rip commented. "She said enough to make me curious about this woman who's going off to Spokane. I'd be surprised if—under cover—someone hasn't sold out to Swayne. A connection of that kind would do more for him than all the spies he could send into the basin. These folks might as well ask Swayne himself to come to their meetings."

"We got a good lead from her. Mebbe we can run it down before evenin'— That crack she made about Matt Cameron was as plain as print."

"Sure," Rainbow agreed. "Cameron's boy was one of that bunch last night."

They got a cool reception at the next ranch. A boy in his early teens rushed out of the house as they turned into the yard. "Stop that noise!" he yelled at Rip. "We can go to town for what we need!"

"Sorry," Rainbow called back. "Someone sick?"

"That ain't none of yore business," the youngster said bluntly.

The partners caught a glimpse of a young woman at one of the windows. She stepped out into the yard a moment later. "Will you please go?" she asked, her pretty face pinched with anxiety. "There's nothing we need."

"Didn't mean to bother yuh," Grumpy told her, swinging the team, adding for Rainbow's ears, "Can you git a flash at that horse and buggy in back of the house?"

"I saw it, Grump. Doctor, no doubt. Chances are that one of those boys who was shot up last evening lives here. Don't turn your head now, but that kid has just forked a bronc and is high-tailing it across the range."

"Reckon you know what that means," the little one muttered. "They'll know we're comin' before we strike the next ranch."

They made a number of stops during the morning and met with a cool reception. Grumpy's adroit attempts to learn the identity of the rancher's wife who was going visiting in Spokane failed completely.

Noon found them in the heart of the basin. Medicine River had begun its long swing to the east some distance back and they could determine its course now only by the distant willow brakes that marched along with its every turning. Just off the road, a big cottonwood offered shade and coolness, and they pulled up for a noonday bite to eat.

Grumpy's good humor of the morning was fading fast. "I been tryin' every trick in the book to git these folks to open up," he complained bitterly as he brewed a pot of coffee. "They close up like clams if you even so much as hint that they might be gittin' a double cross from one of their own crowd."

"You know why we're not getting anywhere, don't you?" Rainbow queried.

"That boy?" the little one shot back, glancing up as he squatted on his toes by the little squaw fire.

"Yeh. I figure he's been ahead of us all morning, tipping people off not to have anything to say to us." In a lighter tone he said, "It'd be mighty slim pickings for us if we were depending on the profits of this business to get us something to eat. If those beans are hot, let's have a plateful."

Their luck took a decided turn for the better that afternoon. At the second place at which they stopped, an elderly woman and her daughter came out. They asked about old Caleb.

"He had to give up the wagon," Grumpy told them. "Full of rhematiz. He's down in Californy now, enjoyin' the sunshine."

"Too bad," the mother said. "He was sech a nice man. But if it ain't rhematiz, it's somethin' else, I allus say."

This was an obvious reference to her daughter, who appeared thin and sickly.

They made several small purchases. The little one helped them out of the wagon.

"That's a bad cough yore daughter's got, ma'am," he said sympathetically. Seeing that the two women had no men folks about led him to hope that he could get them to talk. "A change of climate for a few weeks would do her a world of good. Don't cost so much to run out to Spokane or the Coast."

"We can put the money to better use," the mother said tartly. "I'd like to have Jennie take a long trip; but we can't afford it jest now; I don't see how Elvira Twilley can."

"Oh, Mother, she hasn't gone yet," the daughter protested wearily.

"She told Lucy Talbert she was goin'. Buyin' a new outfit fer the trip, too." The old woman's faded eyes flashed indignantly. " 'Queer,' Lucy said it was, and I agree with her."

"Reckon the Twilleys have a big place," Grumpy pursued guilelessly. "Money comes in easy?"

"Eph Twilley a big place?" the woman cackled scornfully. "The only thing big about Eph Twilley is his mouth. Lissen to him and yuh might think he owned Nazareth Basin. But jedge for yorself— Next place up the road on the right."

Grumpy didn't risk a glance at Rip; he knew they had the information they wanted.

"We hit the jackpot that time," Rainbow said as they drew away. "Sounds like Twilley is Swayne's man. I hope we find him at home."

Their first glimpse of the shabby, neglected house and the littered yard confirmed their suspicions. Everywhere they looked, there was evidence that Eph Twilley was a lazy, shiftless man and long a stranger to prosperity.

Before they got through the gate Eph bounced out of the house, a gun in his hand. "Git out!" he screeched. "I ain't allowin' no strangers on my place!"

The partners sized him up at once for a fat, lazy braggart, in his late forties. Even at a distance he had the smell of the barnyard about him.

"By grab, yo're shore hostile," Grumpy growled back. "Can't a peddler try to make a livin' without havin' a gun shoved in his face?"

"Let him go," Rainbow urged, artfully, accompanying his words with a deprecatory movement of his hand. "We heard along the road it would be a waste of time to stop at the Twilleys'. Back up the team and we'll be on our way. No use embarrassing a man by showing him bargains if he ain't got the cash to buy 'em."

The angry flush that whipped into Twilley's beefy face told Rip the dig about money had found its mark.

"Where the hell did yuh git that talk?" Eph growled. "I got a dollar to spend if I want!" he boasted. "Before I'm through, I'll show some of these blabbin' wimmen around this basin where they git off!"

"Eph, what you arguin' about out there?" came a querulous feminine demand from the house.

"Jest a couple peddlers!" Twilley answered.

"Well, don't you buy nothin'!" he was ordered. "I'll git what I need in Spokane!"

Twilley cursed the woman under his breath for that careless remark, and his shifty eyes were suddenly troubled.

Rainbow gave him a deceivingly apologetic nod. "Reckon what we heard about you being broke was just spite talk. We get an earful of it every day on the wagon. A trip to Spokane takes money."

It gave Grumpy his cue. "Wish we could pick up a little. No one's buyin' much, I can tell yuh; folks is too worried about all this trouble that's comin' at 'em. Glad to see yuh all stickin' together. Reckon Swayne will find he's got a fight on his hands."

"He shore will if folks lissen to me!" Twilley snarled. He felt he was on safer ground now, and without being aware of it, he looked relieved. "We'll have to shoot it out, and the sooner the better," he went on, lowering his gun. "Time's past for the palaverin' Matt Cameron's doin'. It ain't goin' to settle a thing." He came up to the wagon and put his foot on a wheel hub. "I didn't mean to be so hostile," he declared confidentially, "but a man's gotta be careful these days; can't tell when yo're talkin' to one of Swayne's spies."

He was full of exaggerated threats against Noah Swayne and what he personally proposed to do about it. The partners let him exhaust himself with his coarse, loudmouthed ranting. They had known other men who had sold out their own cause and resorted to these same tactics in order to throw suspicion away from themselves.

When Twilley was satisfied that he had impressed them with his hatred of Swayne and all that that individual stood for, he was ready for the partners to pull away. Rainbow had other ideas.

"You want to look out for a double cross, Eph. Swayne's got money. He'll spend some of it to make a traitor of one of you."

The man's head jerked up involuntarily and behind their mounds of fat his eyes were dark with alarm.

"If the man's caught—Lord help him!" Grumpy observed somberly. "If I read these basin folks right, they'll string him up to the first tree."

Twilley nodded. Sparring for time to collect himself, he produced a slab of tobacco and sank his teeth into it. After rolling the chew around in his mouth, he said, "I'd be the fust one to say string the skunk up. But that ain't likely to happen; as yuh said, we're all stickin' together." He turned his head to spit and without meeting Rainbow's eyes, he said, "What gave yuh the idear? Yuh ain't heard nuthin', have yuh?"

He put the question as casually as he could, but he was hanging on Rip's answer.

"I wouldn't say we'd heard anything—just hints. Takes just a whisper to get such things going. If a man starts spending more money than he was figured to have, he'll have some questions to answer."

A look touched Twilley's broad face that tightened his cheeks, and there was no missing the quick stab of fear that ran through him. He took his foot down from the wheel and stepped back, a hard set to his mouth.

"Where yuh aimin' to put up for the night?" he inquired.

"Nazareth—or just beyond," Rip answered.

"There's a good spot two miles north of town—wood and water to hand. Peddlers allus camp there."

The partners thanked him for the tip and drove away. Twilley stood there watching them until they were a hundred yards up the road. Grumpy glanced back to see him darting into the house.

"We ain't see the last of that gent," the little one growled. "His mouth snapped shut like an empty rattrap when you made that crack about spendin' money."

Rainbow smiled. "I could see what he was thinking written all over his face. He'll be after us tonight. He's not going to have us doing any more talking."

"Good grief!" Grumpy exploded. "You mean you was askin' for trouble?"

"Why not? Twilley is the rat in this woodpile. We'll be ready for him."

Ahead of them the partners could see the westering sun gilding the white steeple of Nazareth's Methodist church as it was about to disappear behind the Medicine River Range, far across the basin.

"A purty little town and mighty peaceful-lookin', sittin' out there on the plain like that," Grumpy commented. "White church steeple and the streets lined with the trees—you might think you was back in Indiana or Illinois, but for the mountains."

"We're not apt to find it as peaceful as it looks," Rainbow reminded. "If Mei-lang is all right, and trouble doesn't pile up for us, we'll pull out of Nazareth by dark."

They pretended not to notice the unfriendly attention they attracted as they drove down the town's main street. They passed the wooden courthouse, and adjoining it, the sheriff's office. A youngish man, a silver star pinned on his vest, sat outside the door. He scrutinized them carefully.

"That was the Law," Grumpy muttered. "Reckon he'll recognize us the next time he sees us."

Several doors beyond the post office a crude sign, in Chinese red, the letter N upside down, directed them to Johnny Wong's restaurant. That side of the street appeared to be the popular one, as far as the hitchracks were concerned. Unable to find a vacant space, Grumpy pulled across the road.

Rainbow got down and waited for him to tie the team. Though the wagon stood at an angle to the restaurant door, it did not prevent him from seeing a man step out and cross the sidewalk to his horse. Sight of him had an electric effect on the tall man. To make sure he couldn't be seen, he stepped close to the side of the wagon and pulled Grumpy in with him.

"What's the idea?"

"Across the way, Grump! He's getting into the saddle.

Recognize him?"

"By Joe, I shore do!" the little one grunted in smothered excitement. "Pete Cleary! We goin' to stop him?"

Rainbow said no, and they watched Cleary jog out of town and head across the basin, with Grumpy bristling and growling to himself.

"Get it off your chest," Rip told him.

"That wasn't no way to play it! We coulda grabbed him!"

"It was the only way," the tall man said flatly. "If Cleary's here, so are Slade and Fanin— Mei-lang had the right hunch. If you're ready, we'll walk into the restaurant now. And remember we're not armed."

CHAPTER FOURTEEN

THOUGH MEI-LANG RECOGNIZED the partners as they came through the door she remained seated on her high stool behind the desk and gave them the blank, disinterested glance the Chinese manage so well when occasion demands.

In Johnny Wong's establishment the customers found their own table. Rip selected one near the desk. The hour was late for supper and there were only two other diners, young men, cowboys, judging by their talk and attire. Grumpy put on his spectacles and studied the soiled, handwritten menu. The menu was in keeping with the other appointments of the shabby little restaurant.

"A steak, fried potatoes, and coffee for me," the little one announced.

Rainbow nodded. "That'll do me, too."

Minutes passed before a fat, grinning, middle-aged Chinese waddled forth from in back to take their order. It was Wong himself. Mei-lang left the desk and walked back into the kitchen.

"You wait ten minute," Wong told the partners. "Steak cook to order." Bending over Rainbow, he gave the tall man a knowing wink. "You likee wash up while you wait, place in kitchen."

"We certainly would," Rip said, understanding perfectly.

In the kitchen they found Mei-lang and Cheng Bow waiting for them. The latter was hard put to maintain his Oriental calm in his delight at seeing them again.

"I expected you days ago," Mei-lang said tensely.

"We drove all the way from Billings," Rainbow explained. "We had to take it easy or give our game away. Are you all right?"

"Of course. No one has questioned our being here." She wore no make-up, and her costume was intentionally ill-fitting; but there was no concealing her exquisite features and intelligent, beautiful eyes. "It's fortunate you did not come in a moment earlier—Pete Cleary just left the restaurant." The surprise she expected was not forthcoming.

"I know; we saw him from across the street," said Rip. "Slade and Fanin can't be far away."

"That was my thought, Rainbow. This is the second time he's been in. Cheng Bow saw him on the street the other day and recognized him at once. He's well known in Nazareth. He's been in and out of the basin for years, breaking horses and riding for different stockmen. He says he's working on some ranch up in the mountains now."

"He ain't comin' to town to see the sights," Grumpy observed pointedly. "He's got some business here. Have you got an idea what it is, Mei-lang?"

"I'm not sure. The other day he stayed only a few minutes; this evening, he took his time with his supper and when he finished eating, he sat at the table for a long time reading a newspaper. I had the feeling that he wasn't interested in the newspaper; that he was waiting for someone."

"Did he speak to anyone?" Rip asked.

"No, he sat by himself. Across from him four men were eating. Ranch people. I've come to know some of them by sight. About fifteen minutes ago an acquaintance of theirs came in and joined them at the long table. He was loud, coarse-mouthed. The others tried to get him to lower his voice—they were talking about Swayne and the fight they have on their hands—but he could be heard all over the place. It made me wonder if that wasn't his way of getting a message across to Cleary. Everybody knows the cowmen are having meetings, but when and where they meet is kept a secret. I heard the man say—and I'm sure Cleary did—'We ought to have a big turnout at Matt's place tonight. I reckon it will be nine o'clock before we get down to business.' I glanced at Cleary. He was looking at his paper, but he was listening."

"Yo're dang tootin' he was!" Grumpy declared with conviction. "Meetin' tonight at Matt Cameron's at nine o'clock—that was the message Cleary was in here to git!"

"I'd say that was pretty obvious," Rip agreed. "What happened after that, Mei-lang?"

"The five men left together. A few minutes later, Cleary walked out."

Rainbow asked her to describe the man who had done the talking. It confirmed the partners' surmise.

"Was his name Eph Twilley?" the tall man queried.

"Eph something, they called him—"

"Twilley, sure enough," Rip said soberly. "With the basin men gathered at Cameron's ranch, Swayne's gang will have the coast clear. They'll strike hard somewhere. We better get back to the table. We'll stick around till we're alone out there."

The partners found the food good. They were hungry, and they ate heartily. The two cowboys strolled out, giving them the restaurant to themselves.

Mei-lang was back behind the desk again. Without leaving her post, she said, with undisguised anxiety, "Where will you be tonight?"

"We expected to camp along the road, a couple miles above town," Rip said. "I'd like to tip Cameron off, but that's out of the question."

"Cheng could take a message—"

"No, that would be just as risky. If he got caught, he'd have to explain what he was doing that far from Nazareth. We're not in a position to do any explaining just yet."

"There ain't much we could tell him," the little one asserted. "We don't know where trouble is goin' to hit tonight."

"There was trouble last night—down on the river," Mei-lang told them, keeping an eye on the door. "Two young men were wounded. One of them may die. They were riding with other boys, a dozen or more. They learned that two men were in the basin, trying to buy the Henderson ranch for Swayne. The boys caught up with them and ran them out."

"We know all about that," came from Grumpy. "We had front-row seats. Was them fellers killed?"

"I don't know," Mei-lang murmured soberly. "No one has anything to say about that end of it." Her shoulders stiffened without warning. "Be careful," she said quickly; "this is the sheriff coming in."

The partners recognized the youngish man—they judged him to be in his middle thirties—who had looked them over so carefully as they drove past the sheriff's office. He had a strong, determined face and, in a masculine way, was a rather handsome man. His manner was pleasant as he nodded impersonally to Mei-lang and came up to the table.

"I'm Lin Messenger," he said. "I don't mean to hurry you. When you get through with your supper, drive down to the office; I want to have a little talk with you."

His tone was strictly official and on the stern side, but deep in his blue eyes Rip thought he caught an obscure amusement.

"Anything important?" the tall man asked.

"No—I just want to ask you a few questions."

That was all. He turned and went out. Mei-lang was quick to ask, "What do you suppose he wants, Rainbow?"

"Just the routine questioning, I imagine. He's entitled to know who we are and where we're going and so forth. Or it may be something about what happened last night. If you see us drive out of town, you'll know everything's all right."

When he paid the check, his hand closed on hers impulsively and the light that warmed his eyes told her better than words how much she meant to him. "You've been right all the way, Mei-lang. We want Slade, and we'll try to even our score with Swayne, too. The law can't touch him for what happened down in Idaho, but he put up the money that was responsible for the trouble we had. We won't forget that."

"And you'll keep in touch with me?" she asked, a little catch in her voice.

"We won't be far away," he promised.

The partners got on the wagon and turned back to the sheriff's office. Messenger was waiting for them, and after they entered, he closed the door.

"So you're a couple peddlers, eh?" he said, with a chuckle. "Sit down and make yourselves to home."

The partners found the little boxlike office, with its battered desk, the old chairs, legs wired, the bare walls, even the fly-specked calendar, familiar enough; they had known a hundred like it. They found nothing familiar about Messenger's manner or approach.

"Looks serious—closing the door," Rip remarked.

Messenger smiled briefly. "Just a precaution. We won't be disturbed. This peddling business—you're new at it, aren't you?"

"Depends on what you call new," was the tall man's smoothly evasive answer.

The sheriff let that pass. "I knew you were in the basin. I saw where you camped last night. There was a gun fight below you, a mile or so."

"We heard some shooting," Rip admitted. "There's nothing we can tell you about it."

"I don't imagine there is. It doesn't concern me; it was beyond my jurisdiction. County line runs through there." He leaned back in his chair and his glance ran from Rip to Grumpy and back. "They say it's a small world," he said grinning. "I guess this proves it."

"What's so funny about all this?" the little one jerked out, thoroughly irked and not of a mind to conceal the fact.

"Finding the two of you in those old rags, with a week's stubble on your chins." Messenger shook his head, as though he found it hard to believe. "Rainbow Ripley and Grumpy Gibbs! I thought I recognized you when you passed about an hour ago. In Wong's place, when I came face to face with you, I knew I wasn't mistaken."

"Who are you?" Rip snapped, sitting up stiffly.

"I'm Lin Messenger, sure enough. I wouldn't expect you to remember me. But you used to pass my desk every time you walked into the Wells Fargo detective bureau in Denver to see Jim McBride."

"By grab, yo're right!" Grumpy declared, giving the young sheriff a piercing squint. "I remember you now—

Yo're a long way from Denver. What are you doin' up in this neck of the woods?"

"This is my home range," Messenger replied. "When I left here, I left my heart behind, as the saying goes. She wrote me that her old man thought he could wrangle this job for me if I came home. That was about a year ago, long before all this trouble started. Naturally, I'm wondering what the two of you are doing in Nazareth. Don't tell me you're working for Noah Swayne?"

"No," Rainbow answered, weighing the advantages against the disadvantages of this surprising development. "We're after three men wanted for murder. We have good reason to believe they are among the gun slingers Swayne is turning loose on you folks. We had hoped to be around here a week or two before our identity became known. That's why we came in as a couple peddlers."

"You went to a lot of trouble. It was a smart trick; but I'm afraid it wasn't smart enough. There's a rumor flying around that you're working for Swayne."

Grumpy was about to let out a blast when the tall man cut in ahead of him. "We know where that started, Lin. If things work out as we expect, we may be able to tell you more about it tomorrow. Do you know Matt Cameron well?"

Messenger laughed. "I ought to. He got me elected; and I'm going to marry his daughter."

"Then you can do us a favor. I want you to see him and tell him who we are, and why we're here. You can also tell him that his fight is our fight, as we see it. We'll do everything we can to help the basin men. Would you do that?"

"Sure! He'll be tickled to death to have the two of you on his side."

"Could you get to him tonight?"

Messenger hesitated. "It's a long ride; but I could go up if it's that important."

"It's very important. We know there's going to be a meeting at his house this evening. I don't suppose you ever attend the meetings?"

The sheriff shook his head. "I'd like to take a hand in this fight; but I've got to keep out of it, or turn in my badge."

"That's true," Rip agreed. "But you see Cameron; tell him to look out for trouble tonight. I don't know where it's going to hit you folks, or what it's going to amount to; but something's coming off. If he can get by without disclosing our names for the present, we'll appreciate it."

"And he'll be helpin' himself," the little one added.

Rainbow had decided not to say anything to Messenger about Cleary or Eph Twilley at present. As for Mei-lang and Cheng Bow, he hoped it would never be necessary to reveal why they were in Nazareth.

"I better get started," Lin volunteered. "Where you boys putting up for the night?"

"We understand there is a campground north of town that most peddlers use," Rip told him. "We figured—"

"I wouldn't pull in there!" Messenger interjected gravely. "You'll be safer right here in town. You get out in the basin a couple miles and you're apt to have visitors during the night."

With the faintest of smiles, Rainbow said, "We'll be disappointed if we don't."

"Oh, I see—" The sheriff was not at all sure that he did. "Well," he continued rather dubiously, "you know your own business. When do you expect to see Matt?"

"Sometime tomorrow, if possible," said Rip.

By whipping up the team the partners reached the spot where Eph Twilley had advised them to spend the night before the long summer twilight had completely faded. Following old wagon tracks, they pulled off to the right of the road for several hundred yards, where tangled willows screened a small creek. Along it, they saw the blackened embers of old campfires.

"Been used a lot," Grumpy commented. "Wood and water, jest as Twilley said; and good graze for the team."

They unhitched the horses and picketed them quickly. That done, they built a fire.

"We'll let it burn, so he'll know where to look for us," said Rainbow. "Soon as it gets a bit darker, we'll get our side guns out of the wagon and crawl off into the shadows. I don't imagine we'll have to wait long; he'll figure to get through with us and go on to the meeting."

They had gotten over their surprise at meeting Lin Messenger. Both were of the opinion that it gave them an unexpected ace in the hole.

"What do we do with Twilley when he starts bushwhackin' at us?" the little one demanded as he shoved his .45 under his belt. "This is a purty spot, but I don't aim to remain here permanent."

"We'll get around in back of him, Grump, and jump him. When we get him tied up, we'll toss him into the wagon and pull out for Matt Cameron's ranch. If we get there before the meeting breaks up, we'll give him a chance to talk himself out of the hole he's in."

"They'll hang him, Rip—"

"Maybe they will—if he refuses to talk," Rainbow murmured grimly. "But Cameron seems to have a level head. I believe if Twilley tells what he knows he'll just be run out of the basin. We better get away from the fire now."

They had taken only a few steps when they were ordered to throw up their hands. It was a young voice, and it came from the willows. The partners looked around and found movement in every direction. It told them all too plainly that they had been watched for some minutes.

"We better oblige," Rip muttered. "These are the same kids we saw last night."

Off to their left Eph Twilley walked out into firelight, gun in hand. "Bring 'em over to the wagon, boys!" he cried. "Bust 'em if they make a wrong move!"

In a moment or two the partners found themselves surrounded. Twilley climbed into the wagon and tossed out their saddles and rifles. "There yuh are!" he roared. "They ain't no more peddlers than I be! They're workin' for Swayne! He sent 'em into the basin to spy on us!"

These reckless young partisans, some of them barely out of their teens, were not hard to convince. Rip realized that was why Twilley had turned to them for support instead of calling on older heads.

"We know what to do with them," said one. He spoke with the authority that comes with leadership; a tall, black-haired, handsome boy. With a coolness that belied his years, he disarmed the partners. He said, "If you got anything to say for yourselves, let's hear it."

"Why waste time talkin', Del?" one of the boys demanded hotly. "Let's get this over with! They wouldn't have rifles and ridin'-gear in their wagon if they was honest-to-God peddlers!"

"You're right," Rainbow spoke up. "Peddling isn't our business; we used it as a dodge to get into the basin without giving our hand away." He gave Twilley a long, chilling glance. "Eph, you look worried. You didn't believe the story you told these boys that we are a couple spies. Now you don't know what to think. Maybe you're asking yourself if you haven't bungled some of Noah Swayne's secret plans."

"Why, yuh dirty hound!" Eph roared, bringing up his gun. "I'll bust yuh for that–"

Del stopped him in time. "Shut up!" he admonished. "I'll do the talking here." And to Rip: "What did you mean by that crack?"

"Twilley wants us rubbed out because he's afraid we've put the finger on him, not because he thinks we're doing any spying. My partner and I have our own ax to grind; but we came to Nazareth to get in this fight on your side. Lin Messenger knows who we are. He'll vouch for us. I suspect one of you boys is Matt Cameron's son. Am I right?"

Del said, "I'm his son. What about it?"

"Lin is at your house right now, telling your father who we are and why we're here. Before you boys wash us out, you better know what your doing."

It had its effect. The boys fell back a step and exchanged uneasy glances with one another.

"Don't yuh believe a word of what he says!" Twilley bellowed. "They're slick talkers, both of 'em!" He knew he had maneuvered himself into a precarious position, and for all his noise, he couldn't conceal the fear that was knifing through him.

Young Del whirled on him savagely. "For the second time, I'm telling you to close your trap, Eph! We're going to get to the bottom of this. If Lin knows these men and says they're okay, that'll be good enough for us. But I ain't taking their word for it; I want Lin to say so. To be on the safe side, I'll thank you for your gun."

"No, yuh don't!" Twilley cried. "Yuh ain't takin' my gun!"

A boy slipped up behind the man and shoved the nose of his .44 into Eph's back. "Drop it!" he grunted. Twilley could do nothing but oblige.

Young Cameron turned to the partners and ordered them to hitch the team. "We're taking you up to the ranch."

"I'm afraid Lin will be gone before we get there," said Rainbow. "He carried a message from us to your father, telling him to cut the meeting short, so the men could get home. Thanks to your friend Twilley, hell's going to break loose somewhere tonight. He tipped Pete Cleary off about the time and place of the meeting."

"Say, what are you givin' us?" one of the boys lashed out incredulously. "We know Pete! He's all right!"

"He's a gun slick—wanted for murder—and back in the basin only because he's running with the rest of Swayne's thugs." Rip wasn't holding back now. "With everyone up at the Camerons', the basin is wide open for a raid—Twilley can tell you where they're going to hit you. Make him talk."

In some intangible way, Del and the others knew they were hearing the truth. Eph's reaction to Rip's charge confirmed it. Twilley had never been a man of any consequence in the community. Years ago, he had been put down as a lazy, lying braggart. Though his honesty had never been questioned, under the present circumstances, his dubious reputation suddenly made it easy to believe the worst.

Several of the boys started to rush at him. Del drove

them back. "I'll make him talk," he jerked out hotly. "Come on, Twilley, open up!"

"It's all lies!" Eph whined. "I didn't say nuthin' to Pete Cleary!"

"I believe you're the liar!" young Cameron rapped. "You'll talk, Eph, or you won't leave here alive! Where they hitting us?"

"I dunno, I tell yuh!" Twilley's voice cracked, it was pitched so high. "There ain't goin' to be no raid, I know of!"

"No," Grumpy screeched. "Listen to that! They're in Nazareth right now—shootin' up the town!"

In the moment they listened, the night wind carried to their ears the unmistakable rattle of distant gunfire.

"There you are," Rainbow said tensely. "You boys have been itching to get into this fight. Now you've got your chance. Tie up Twilley and one of you stay here to guard him; the rest of us will high-tail it for Nazareth."

"Right!" Del agreed without hesitating, though he knew he was handing over his leadership to Rainbow. "We're riding with you."

CHAPTER FIFTEEN

RAINBOW CALLED A HALT at the edge of town and listened to the rattle of gunfire. It had a pattern, rising violently, then dropping to scattered shots and swelling again in an angry crescendo. He was not only convinced that the raiders were in Nazareth in strength, but that they were riding up and down the main street at will, first in one direction and then the other.

"Most of the stores have flat roofs," he said to young Cameron. "Can we get up on top of them from the rear?"

"There's alleys in back. Most of the buildings have outside stairs."

"Good! We'll go up the alley on this side. A couple of you get up on the post office roof. The rest of you climb up where you can; my partner and I'll take the Chinese restaurant."

Johnny Wong's little establishment was housed in a two-story building, the restaurant on the ground floor and the living-quarters above. The partners ran up the back stairs and got as far as the second floor and could go no farther. Inside, not a light was burning, upstairs or down.

Cheng had heard them run up the steps. Not being able to recognize them in the darkness, he leveled a gun at them, thinking they were about to break in, when Rip cried, "Mei-lang! Cheng! Open the door!"

The sounds that followed from within told him the door had been barricaded. Someone lit a candle as furniture was pulled aside. When the door was flung open, Mei-lang stood there, her lips parted with anxiety and her face pale against the midnight blackness of her hair. She had a silk robe wrapped tightly about her. The robe and her heelless slippers made her look slim and small. Johnny Wong and his wife came in and stood behind her.

"Don't be alarmed," Rip said reassuringly, "you'll be all right if you go back to your bedrooms and lie down on the floor till this thing is over. How do we get up on the roof?"

"There is a trap door in my room," Cheng answered. "Can I go up with you, Mr. Ripley?"

"You stay here, Cheng. Barricade the door again. If anyone tries to bust in, kill him. Where is the trap?"

Mei-lang clutched his arm. "Rainbow—don't expose yourself! They'll see you on the roof—there's fourteen or more. They've shot out the street lamps and shattered every window on the street."

"Grump and I are not alone; we've got help," he told her.

Cheng Bow stopped as he was hurrying from the room. "Mr. Ripley—Slade is with them; and so are Fanin and Cleary. I saw them."

"All right!" the little one growled. "Let's git up there! If we can't take 'em alive, we'll take 'em dead!"

There was light from the street as they climbed out on the roof; burning oil from a broken street lamp had set the plank sidewalk afire. With hoofs pounding, the raiders raced past, firing shot after shot through the already shattered store windows, apparently with no other purpose in mind than to further cow the town. When they reached the end of the street without drawing a shot from the roof tops, Rip sighed in relief.

"A shot or two might have scared them off, Grump. Now, they'll come back, and this time they'll smell a different brand of gun smoke."

It was only a minute or two before they came racing back, raking the street with gunfire. They had taken Nazareth by surprise, and after the first few minutes had had things all their own way. They were now so confident they could do as they pleased that they paid little attention to the first little volley that came from the roof of Spangler's hardware store, a distance of a city block to the west of the restaurant. They peppered the cornice with slugs and continued down the street. But guns roared from the roof next door, and the next.

One of the raiders went down. The partners saw him

pitch out of the saddle and hit the dust. Consternation gripped the others. All were easy targets from the roofs. In their haste to escape the fate that had overtaken their fallen companion, they drove their broncs in under the wooden awnings, knocking down some of the posts on which the awnings rested.

"Slade—on the gray hoss!" the little one grunted.

He fired, but he was a split second too late, the slug missing as Slade drove under the awnings, and barely nicking his gray horse.

The partners recognized his bull-like voice as he barked at the others to hug the buildings and go down the sidewalk. It was evidence enough that he was in charge.

Away they went at a driving gallop, the loose planks sending up a clatter. When they reached the last of the stores, they swung out into the open street. Out of range there, they pulled up, apparently debating the wisdom of returning to the attack.

A faint beating, no louder at first than the pelting of driving rain, pulled Rainbow's attention away from them and to the north. What he saw had a galvanizing effect. "Grump, look! Off there to the north!"

"By gravy, it's the men from the meetin'! Thirty—forty of 'em!"

The newcomers were riding hard. Spread out in a long, thin line, they poured over the rolling plain. It was like a wave rolling across a sandy beach.

Though Slade and his cohorts were unaware of what impended, in the stillness that had descended on Nazareth it could be only a matter of minutes before the drumming of hoofs cried a warning to them. Hoping to gain time for the basin men, the partners began firing into the air. From their perch on the roofs, Del and the other boys saw that help was on the way, and when Rip and Grumpy started their guns to bucking, they understood why, and followed suit.

The stratagem was successful. With the night raucous with gunfire again, the basin men reached the edge of town before they were detected. As they roared down the street,

Swayne's forces turned and fled without waiting to fire a shot.

Lin Messenger was among the men from the meeting. He pulled up across from the restaurant as the others flashed past in pursuit of the raiders and attempted to put out the fire that, by now, had burned across the sidewalk and was licking at the door of the drugstore. Rip stood up and called to him.

"We'll be down in a minute and give you a hand, Lin!"

Del and the others were standing up, too. Messenger gave them a startled glance. "I be danged!" he jerked out. "How in hell did you fellas get up there?"

"We git around some!" Grumpy told him.

On the way down Rainbow stopped for a word with Mei-lang. "It's all over," he said. "Slade was bossing this job. He's on the run now. He may not get away—"

"Rainbow—there's a man lying in the road—"

He nodded. "I know—one of Slade's bunch. It'll be a miracle if none of these Nazareth folks got it. I must go now."

He took her in his arms briefly and felt her lips warm and strong on his mouth.

Pop Weedon, the proprietor of the drugstore had limped out with a bucket of water. He had been standing behind the counter when a slug struck him in his left leg, above the knee. Rip grabbed the bucket and refilled it several times before the blaze was extinguished.

"The town sure got shot up!" Messenger muttered, glancing up and down the street. "We got here as quickly as we could—"

"Lin, what about that bunch of thugs? Where will they run to?"

"They'll swing around town and line out across the basin."

Del and his friends had joined them. They didn't find it necessary to ask Lin if he knew the partners.

"Before we do anythin' else, let's have a look at that gent layin' in the road," the little one suggested.

When they reached the body, Messenger turned the dead

man over and had a look at him.

"Wal!" Grumpy exclaimed in a sepulchral tone. "Joe Fanin. We won't have to bother with gittin' him back to Mustang Gap!"

Messenger glanced at Rip. "You know him, eh?"

"He's one of the three we're after, Lin."

Nazareth was coming to life again; men and some women ran down from their homes above the stores. Others, still fearful, draped themselves out of upper-story windows and called down for information about the fighting.

A hasty check of the casualties revealed that almost a dozen people had been injured, most of them by flying glass. Fortunately, no one was seriously wounded.

Rainbow walked aside with Lin and told him what had transpired back at the wagon, and the facts about Eph Twilley. The recital stunned the sheriff.

"I don't know what to say," he declared bitterly. "I've known Eph a long time. He's always a liar and a braggart; I wouldn't have believed he could be low enough to stab us in the back— We better go after him, Rip. I'm not sure there's anything I can charge him with; but I'll lock him up for his own good; when folks learn what he's been up to, some of them will stretch his neck if they get their hands on him."

"After what's happened tonight, I'll have to agree with you," said Rainbow. "I don't know how strong your jail is. If you get him locked up, is there any chance a mob can take him away from you?"

"Nobody will take him away from me," Messenger said thinly. "I don't have a deputy. I use Sam Thompson, when I need help. Between the two of us we'll hang on to Eph— Does Del and the rest of these kids know who you are?"

"No, we didn't have to tell them. I said you knew us and would say we are okay. Del was going to put it up to you. He seems to have convinced himself that the little fellow and I were telling the truth. They'll insist on going up to get Twilley with us. Don't say anything about arresting him. We'll pull that on them at the last minute. There'll only be the three of us, but I figure we can handle the situation."

They rode out of Nazareth a few minutes later without any hint of what was happening out across the basin. There had been some shooting, but the night was peaceful again.

"They must be getting into the hills by now," Lin remarked. "If it's turned into a fight, we wouldn't hear it down here."

"You don't sound very hopeful," the little one declared.

"I'm not, Grumpy. Front runners can usually travel faster than the men who are chasing them—especially when you got a bunch as big as Matt has with him. My worry right now is to have Eph locked up before they get back."

There was talk among the boys as they rode back to the wagon—talk from which the partners and Messenger were excluded. The latter were in no doubt as to the tenor of it.

"They ain't goin' to let us have Twilley," Grumpy told Lin. "These kids smell blood."

"There won't be much of an argument," Messenger said confidently.

"There won't be no argument at all if they pull a surprise and git the drop on us—"

"We'll beat them to it," Rainbow spoke up. "Be ready when we get down from the saddle."

Such concerns went flying out of their heads when they rode up to the wagon; Eph Twilley was gone, and so was one of old Caleb's aged horses. It spelled calamity for the partners. The lines in Grumpy's grizzled face deepened.

"Rip, the jig is up if he gits to Slade with what he knows about us—"

The tall man could only nod in silent agreement.

Van Hibbard, who had been left to guard Eph, lay stretched out on the ground. Hearing them, he managed to sit up groggily. At once, Del and the others began to bombard him with questions.

"You won't get anything out of him that way," Rip protested, his voice sharp with annoyance. "He got a bad crack on the head and he's been out cold for some time. Fetch some water and we'll help him to pull himself together."

It was some minutes before Van could give them a coherent account of what had happened.

"I don't know how he got his hands free," he said. "After you fellows left, he sat here by the fire, cursing and whining. I didn't have much to say to him. I wanted a drink. Before I went down to the crick to get it, I made sure he was well tied. When I came back, he tripped me. He was on top of me in a second and hit me on the head with something—a rock, I reckon."

Grumpy held up a charred piece of rope. "There's yore answer. When you went down to the crick, Twilley managed to git some coals out of the fire and brought his hands down over 'em and burned the rope he was tied with. After he'd knocked you out, he got his legs free."

"No doubt," Rip agreed. He was thinking fast. "He couldn't hope to get far on our old nag— Where could he find a good bronc?"

"Sam Watoon's place is the nearest—a couple miles up the basin," Messenger told him.

"That's where he'd head for." The tall man turned to Del. "You get up to Watoon's. If Twilley's there, grab him; if not, find out which way he went and ride him down. And don't make the mistake of taking the law into your own hands when you catch up with him."

Messenger would have objected, but Rainbow's glance carried a message that stopped him. The boys mounted quickly and flashed away in the direction of the Watoon ranch.

"I know you're figuring to outsmart them," Lin said sharply, puzzled and nettled as well. "But I don't follow you. If they get their hands on—"

"They won't, if we move fast enough. When Twilley left here, he didn't go that way; he headed for his own place. His wrists are burned; they've got to be taken care of. And he'll need some money and grub before he pulls out of the basin. We'll find him there, Lin."

A single light burned in the kitchen of Eph Twilley's house. Turning off the road, the partners and Messenger approached by way of the barn and the corral. In the yard, they saw the old bay horse that had helped to pull the wagon into Nazareth Basin. The animal was grazing contentedly in the yard.

"You hit the nail on the head, Rip," Messenger muttered. "He may be gone, but he was here."

"He's still here," said Rainbow. "That's a saddled bronc at the kitchen door. We'll wait till Twilley comes out. If we go in after him, he'll put up a fight."

"Inside or out, he'll throw lead at us if he gits the chance," Grumpy warned. "Which way do you figger he'll run, Lin?"

"He won't risk the road. It's my guess he'll try to get across the basin and head into the mountains."

Rip nodded in agreement. "If we're right, he'll have to pass the barn. Suppose we pull up in back of it and wait. If we get to him quick enough, he won't be able to use his gun."

They didn't have long to wait. The kitchen door opened and Eph stepped out. His wife came that far with him. They were snarling at each other. He swung up into the saddle and she slammed the door as he moved away.

Behind the barn, the partners and Messenger heard him jogging down the yard and knew he was riding right into their hands. When he hove into view, they rushed out and had him surrounded before he could even begin to break away.

"What's the idear?" he screeched at Messenger. "I ain't bruk no law! These lyin' skunks yo're travelin' with are makin' a fool of yuh!"

"You'll shut your lip if you know what's good for you," Lin advised grimly. "I'm taking you into Nazareth and locking you up; and that's doing you a favor. A cell is the only place in the basin where you'll be safe tonight. I don't want any gab out of you, Eph; just get moving along."

With Grumpy tagging behind with the old bay in tow, they got Twilley into town and put him behind bars with scarcely anyone being the wiser. It would not have been possible, half an hour later.

"After what's happened tonight, I don't know how much secrecy you boys can hope for," Lin said to the partners. "Certainly none unless you get out of town in a hurry. My advice would be to get back to the crick, hitch up, and go on to the Camerons'. They'll take you in and hide you out—if that's what you want."

"How about you, Lin?" Rip asked. "Will you be all right?"

"Sure! I'll send for Sam. If necessary, the two of us can fort up in here and hold off a mob." A horseman dashed up to the jail and flung himself out of the saddle. "Del—and he's steaming," Messenger muttered. "He's heard something— Let him in."

"That was a damn fine trick, wasn't it?" young Cameron rapped angrily. "Sending us off on a wild-goose chase to Watoon's while you birds pulled out for Twilley's place. You'll have to give him up, Lin."

"Not a chance," Messenger returned coolly. "You made one bad mistake tonight; don't make another. These friends of mine came through for us in a big way. I want you to ride up to their wagon with them and take them to the ranch."

"The old man ain't there," Del objected, not liking the idea at all.

"He will be. Your father knows who these men are. If you knew, you wouldn't be standing there giving me an argument."

Del was not easily persuaded, but in the end he gave in. A few minutes after he and the partners left for the wagon, his father and the big posse returned empty-handed from their pursuit of Slade and his gunmen. When they learned of Twilley's treachery, many of them joined the youngsters in demanding that Messenger give up his prisoner. A score of them descended on the jail. They found Lin and Sam Thompson waiting on the steps.

"Eph stays where he is," Messenger told the crowd. "You know me; you know I won't give him up. Tomorrow, after you've cooled off, you'll thank me for the stand I'm taking."

Some jeered. One raised his voice above the others and

shouted, "You fooled us, too, Messenger! You're as big a damned turncoat as Eph Twilley!"

There was more in the same vein. Matt Cameron forced his way through his followers and got up on the steps beside the sheriff. He was a big man and had lost little of his virility with the passing years. "Lin is right," he told them. "Hanging Eph won't help our cause any; he's done all the damage he can do. So far, we've kept our heads; let's not lose them now."

Though their respect for him was great, they were reluctant to heed his counsel now. "Yo're wrong, Matt!" a wizened little man cried. "We oughta make an example of him! How do we know there ain't other skunks like him amongst us?"

Similar sentiments were expressed by others. Big Matt took them on in turn, and when he finished with them, they turned away, growling in their beards; but they had no argument left.

Finally the crowd began to disperse. Matt stood there with Lin and Sam Thompson until the last man had gone. "That took a heap of palaverin'," he said, chuckling. "They may get their second wind and come back; but I doubt it. What's become of Ripley and his partner?"

"They're on their way up to C Bar with Del," Messenger informed him. "You should find them there when you get home. They saved our bacon tonight, Matt. The town's a mess; but I'm afraid there wouldn't have been anything left of it but for Rip and the little fellow."

Cameron nodded soberly. "It shows you how far Swayne will go to put us out of the basin. I hope I can persuade your friends to see this fight through to the finish with us."

"If I know 'em," Lin said, with a smile, "it won't take much persuasion. They've asked for chips in this game, and they'll play them like they were all big ones."

CHAPTER SIXTEEN

THE PLODDING TEAM moved so slowly that the wagon had just rolled into the C Bar yard when Matt reached the ranch. From the saddle, he reached out and shook hands with the partners, saying, "Lin told me I'd find you here. Get down and come into the house."

"Before we do," said Rip, "I'd like to conceal this outfit somewhere. I don't believe we'll be using it again."

"We can take care of that," Matt assured him. "Del, there's room in the old barn, isn't there?"

"I pushed a hayfork in there the other day. I'll wheel it out. Drive down in back of the bunkhouse," he told Grumpy.

He had the door run back when they got there. With the fork out of the way, the little one backed the wagon into the barn.

"We'll get our saddles and personal belongings in the morning," Rainbow remarked. "There's a little bit of everything in the way of notions in the wagon. You and your womenfolks can help yourselves."

"We'll pay you for anything we can use—"

"No, that isn't necessary. The railroad company is paying all expenses. We figured we'd have to ditch the wagon, sooner or later. It seems to have been money well spent. I don't know whether Lin said anything to you about our plans, but we'd like to make our headquarters with you. We don't want to put you out; we'll bunk with the crew."

"I wouldn't hear of it," Cameron objected. "We've got lots of room in the house. The missus and Vangie will make you comfortable. It's late, but they're still waiting up for me. Come along; we'll go in."

Del's chin went up angrily and the tall man caught the sullen look that clamped itself on the boy's face.

"Everybody is in on the big secret but me," the youngster whipped out sarcastically. "Why are you freezing me out? Am I too young to be trusted? Is that it?"

"You're right, Del," said Rip. "You gave a good account of yourself tonight; you're certainly entitled to know who we are. I'm Rainbow Ripley. This is my partner, George Gibbs."

"What!" Del cried incredulously. "You're Rainbow Ripley and Grumpy Gibbs—the detectives?"

Rip could not refrain from smiling at the boy's surprise. "You don't mean to say you've heard of us?"

"From Lin, a hundred times! When he first came home from Denver, we used to sit around in the evening, shooting the breeze. He often spoke about you and things you'd done. No wonder he told me tonight that I'd keep my mouth shut if I knew who you were."

"Del," his father admonished, "you're to keep what you know to yourself for the present. These gentlemen are not in the basin by accident; they're after some men who happen to be working for Swayne. There doesn't want to be any loose talk."

"If we can keep under cover for a few days, that'll be the extent of it," Grump declared. "The birds we want would have flown the coop tonight if Twilley had got away."

Over the years, several additions had been built on to the original C Bar house. Today it was a rambling, comfortable ranch home, softened by the innumerable touches that only a feminine hand can supply.

Mrs. Cameron was younger than her husband and still an attractive woman, with a sensitive, intelligent face. As for Vangie, Rainbow told himself that she was pretty enough to drag a man back from much farther away than Denver.

"I made some coffee," she said, after the introductions. "I'll bring it in."

"There's cake in the pantry, Vangie," her mother reminded. "The gentlemen might like some. I'm sure Del would."

Without conscious effort, she knew how to make a stranger feel at home under her roof—a gift that few women possess. Though she was anxious to learn what had occurred since the meeting had been called off and the basin men had left C Bar in such haste, she restrained her curiosity, confident that when Matt had settled himself in his favorite chair and lighted his pipe he would speak. His account of the night's happenings was brief, but it satisfied her; and after Vangie came in with the coffee and cake, she excused herself for the night.

"You gentlemen can use the bedroom at the head of the stairs," she told the partners.

Rainbow thanked her and apologized for his appearance and Grumpy's. "We'll shed these rags in the morning, Mrs. Cameron, and make ourselves a little more presentable. And we might as well shave off the whiskers. They don't seem to be much of a disguise; Lin Messenger spotted us at first glance."

Vangie followed her mother upstairs a few minutes later. Del got to his feet.

"I suppose you want me to clear out, too."

"I think so," said his father. "I didn't know till last night, when Billy Moffat and Andy White were brought home wounded from down the river, that Del was ringleader, or even riding with those boys," he continued, addressing the partners. "I've tried to keep him out of this fight. Boys of his age don't have much judgment. They proved it tonight by letting Twilley fool them. But for a miracle, they would have lynched the two of you. They mean well; and they're just as much concerned as any of us. But they're hotheaded and usually do more harm than good."

"That's often true," the tall man agreed. "This whole setup is an old story to us; we've fought similar grabs for power and water a number of times. Always when young fellows of Del's age start riding together and acting on their own, it's because they've been shut out of taking an open hand in the scrap. Treat them like boys, and they'll act like boys. In my opinion, it would be a lot better to treat them as men and make them shoulder a man's responsibilities. After all, this is going to be their country one of these days, Matt. They ought to have a right to fight for it."

Del was so pleased he couldn't repress a little cry of satisfaction. "That's what I been saying for weeks, Rainbow! Give us a chance to do our part—that's all we want!"

Matt smoked his pipe thoughtfully for a few moments. "I hadn't looked at it from that angle," he confessed. "In a way, I can see that it might be better to take them in as full partners rather than to have them running wild on their own."

"That's my idea," said Rainbow. "If it's just the same to you, let Del sit down and hear what we have to say." He focused his attention on young Cameron. "There's just one condition—you boys will have to go along with the organization; attend the meetings and take orders, same as the others."

"You've got my word on that," Del assured him.

Matt spoke at length, reviewing the circumstances that had led up to the present situation. Though the partners were hearing much of it for the first time, they found little that was new in it. All they had to do was substitute other places and other men and the facts added up to the same thing.

Grumpy had been silent an overly long time for him. He spoke up now and what he had to say was pertinent. "The generals say the offense is the best defense. You ain't been playin' it that way, Matt; you've been fightin' a defensive battle. What makes you think you can win out if you play it along those lines?"

"We got time on our side. If we can hold Swayne off long enough he can't win." The boss of C Bar was a formidable-looking figure as the words fell from his iron-willed mouth. "When he jammed his bill through the legislature, I managed to tack an amendment on it. He had one year from the day the governor signed it into law to complete his dam. He's lost two months already. If he started work tomorrow morning, it would take him five to six months to finish."

That Swayne had a deadline to meet was news to the partners. In some measure, it changed the whole picture and compelled them to hastily revamp some of their previously held opinions. Rainbow refused to become optimistic, however.

"It's an advantage we hadn't known about," he said carefully. "If this water project was a legitimate undertaking by an honorable man, work on the dam would have been started at once. On the record, Swayne is a get-rich-quick blackleg. He won't pour a yard of concrete until he's got the land he needs sewed up. I understand he's got to have seventy-five per cent of it before the state will step in and authorize condemnation proceedings on the rest. How much does he have now, Matt?"

"He's got better than two-thirds of what he needs. And that's all he's going to get."

Rip leaned back, shaking his head. "I wish I could agree with you. He's got Twilley's place, of course. He'll keep putting on the pressure. Some folks will weaken—not because they want to; emergencies come up—sickness, death, a desperate need for money. What can a man do? He's up against it; he's got to sell. It could happen to you, or to anyone else. I'm speaking from experience when I tell you you're making a mistake if you put all your eggs in one basket. Time may be running for you. But you can't depend on it. It isn't enough. You've got to bait Swayne into making a mistake." The tall man checked himself and added apologetically, "I'm talking out of turn; it's not my place to tell you what to do."

"That's all right," Cameron told him. "I'm glad to hear anything you've got to say. I agree with most of it. It's mighty tough on a man to have this thing hanging over his head day after day; I go to sleep with it and get up with it on my mind. But I wouldn't say we'd been playing a waiting game. Lord knows that's never been my intention. We've turned Swayne back every time he's come at us until he pulled this raid tonight. If we'd caught up with that bunch, we'd have wiped them out to a man."

His voice had turned grim. Though he kept it down, it filled every corner of the room with its earnestness.

"You made 'em run—that's somethin'," the little one declared belligerently.

"Perhaps it's just as well things ended as they did," said Rip. "They'll be encouraged to try again. They may not come off so lucky the next time. But knocking off a bunch of Swayne's gun slicks is not what I meant when I said we'd have to bait him into a mistake; we've got to be smarter than that—pull off something that will bring Swayne himself into the basin. When we get him involved so he can't back out, we'll pull the rug out from under him." He shook his head and smiled as he saw the unasked question that formed in Matt's eyes. "Don't ask me how we're to do it. I couldn't tell you right now; but we'll figure out something."

They spoke of many things in the hour that they sat there. Rainbow had no hesitancy in naming Ben Slade and Pete Cleary as the men they wanted. In discussing the losing battle Slade had waged against the Denver and Pacific, north of Mustang Gap, and how the trail of the wanted men had led Grumpy and him to Montana and Nazareth Basin, he was careful not to make any reference to Mei-lang.

Before bidding the Camerons good night, Grumpy said, "*How you goin' to explain our bein' here to yore crew,* Matt? They'll want to know who we are."

"Well—I don't suppose there's anything I can do but tell the boys you're a couple men we brought in to help us fight Swayne. Will that do?"

"It will if it's what you told your friends at the meeting," Rip put in. "It won't take them long to discover for themselves that we're a couple detectives. In the meantime, the peddlers we've been pretending to be will have disappeared."

Matt laughed softly. "Reckon we can get away with that."

Bathed, shaved, and attired in their range clothes, the partners presented a changed appearance at breakfast. Word had been brought out from town that the night had passed without further incident after they left.

Over the coffee, Matt said, "I don't know what your

plans are for today, but if you'd like to get acquainted with this end of the basin, I'll be glad to show you around."

"That's one of the first things we want to do," Rip replied. "And Matt—do you know where Swayne plans to cut into the river?"

"He figures he's going to bring the water in across my upper range, not far from where the river comes out of the hills."

"Suppose we ride up there," the tall man suggested. "I'd like to see what he's got in mind."

Matt had a stockman's understandable pride in showing C Bar to the partners, knowing that, as stockmen themselves, they could appreciate its worth.

"You've got the water and grass we don't have in our corner of Wyomin'," Grumpy pointed out, as favorably impressed as he had been on catching his first glimpse of Nazareth Basin.

"And no man's going to spoil it if I can help it," Matt declared solemnly. "C Bar's a small spread for Montana, but what there is of it is first-class; I've been upgrading my cattle for almost twenty years."

"You can see the results," Rainbow told him, gazing at a bunch of white-faced Herefords grazing contentedly near the river. "They're as fat as finished beef."

The gently rolling plain that formed the floor of Nazareth Basin began to pitch upward ever so slightly as it reached out toward the southern foothills of the Medicine River Range. Rip could see where the river broke out of the hills, but he couldn't discern how it got into the basin.

"I seem to hear the river, but I can't see it," he said to Matt.

"It swings along behind that first low ridge ahead," the owner of C Bar explained. "It's not till it gets down east of Nazareth that it flows level with the basin; and right away it begins to cut a little canyon for itself. You saw the lower river, so you know how it is. It would be no trick to tap it up here. If there was any need for us to irrigate, we could do it easily enough."

"Maybe you should have done that very thing," Rainbow remarked thoughtfully. "Legislatures in these Western states usually keep their hands off irrigated lands."

Cameron shook his head. "We're afraid we'd be flooded out if we let the river in. I've seen it rain for four days without letup. No question but what Medicine River should be harnessed; but this isn't the place to do it. Go back in the mountains three or four miles and build a dam. You could control the river the year around and develop just as much power as down here."

"That would be expensive," Grumpy observed.

"Yeh—expensive!" Matt ground out bitterly. "That's the rub! That's why the legislature turned down my bill to make flood control of Medicine River a government project—which is what it should be. Instead, they hand it over to Noah Swayne on a silver platter. The only excuse they could give for voting as they did was that it would save the state some money. It didn't matter that our homes would have to be torn out and we'd be driven off our land. They haven't heard the last of it, I guarantee you; we're still here, and we're going to stay here!"

The lower reaches of the foothills had been timbered off, but so long ago that, unopposed, the mahogany, wild cherry, and alder scrub that had sprung up had grown rank. Grumpy eyed it darkly, telling himself how easily a lurking foe could move back and forth unseen and have a good part of the upper basin under his guns.

It weighed on the little man's mind, and finally he said to Cameron, "Those hills over there to the right—I notice yo're givin' 'em a wide berth, Matt. Did you ever have any trouble up here?"

"Ten days ago or so, the boys found a couple cows that had been shot down. I knew the slugs came from up there. We went in and found so many fresh tracks that I moved all my stuff over to this side of the basin. Farther down, shots have been exchanged with Swayne's gunmen a number of times. They have the run of the mountains. There's good trails where you can get up in the big timber."

"Do you know where they rendezvous?" Rip asked.

"Back in the mountains about eight miles. Place called

Silver Gulch. Some mining activity there years ago. It's been a ghost camp for years."

"Why ain't Messenger run 'em out?" came from the little one.

"His authority doesn't go that far. The sheriff in Buffalo Lodge knows they're there; but he sees things Swayne's way and won't do anything about it. We can climb up to the river here."

It took them only a few minutes to ascend the rocky slope. They found the river running high.

"Storm somewheres in the mountains last night," Grumpy declared, stating the obvious.

"I don't know exactly where he plans to make the cut; but along here somewhere," Matt volunteered.

Rainbow got down and walked back and forth for a hundred yards. Looking down the basin, he was surprised to see how it fell away toward Nazareth. As for making the cut, it appeared to him to be a comparatively easy matter. "He'll have some blasting to do," he mused aloud. "This is solid rock under foot. But a gang of experienced men could do the job in a week. What's that country off to the east? It looks tough."

"It is tough," Cameron answered. "It's out and out badlands when you get in there a couple miles. Every storm cuts it up more. Nothing but sand and catclaw till you hit those mountains you see peeking up on the horizon."

The tall man got back in the saddle. "Too bad the river can't be turned that way—if it has to be turned."

Cameron looked at him askance. "You don't mean that seriously, Ripley?"

"No—but it could be done. You couldn't get away with it, of course; the law would be after you. I'm wondering why Swayne didn't think of it; he'd have had flood control, power, and no trouble."

"I can give you the answer," said Matt. "Buffalo Lodge depends on the river for its water."

Rainbow smiled humbly. "That certainly answers me."

They spent the rest of the morning in the basin. Cameron pointed out the trail that led through the mountains to Silver Gulch. "We chased that bunch as far as this last night," he told the partners. "We thought they sure would take the trail. That's how we lost them; they must have turned off as soon as they reached the hills." He gave them a shrewd, sober glance. "If you have any idea of going into the Gulch, don't go in alone."

"You're dead wrong, Matt," Rainbow said in his quietly positive way as he continued to study the serrated green sky line of the mountains. "If we have to go in, our chances will be better if we go in alone."

They had turned toward home and were halfway across the basin when they saw three men gathered on the gallery of a ranch house. They hailed Cameron at once, their manner urgent.

"John Calvin, Frank Warren, and Buck Winters—three men I can count on to go all the way with me," Matt told the partners. "You better let me make you acquainted; you can depend on them to keep their mouths closed."

"All right," Rip agreed, on sudden impulse. "Perhaps the less mystery there is about us in some quarters, the better."

The strained faces of the three men on the gallery left no doubt of the anxiety that gripped them. It was quickly explained. Buck Winters had just arrived from town with a copy of the previous day's edition of the Buffalo Lodge *Intelligencer*. Over Noah Swayne's name, it carried a full-page ad, stating that construction of the Medicine River dam was about to begin and advising laborers and trained artisans interested in a job to register at his offices at once. Matt's neighbors wanted to know what he made of it.

"I don't know what to say," was Cameron's sober, perplexed answer. "I—I can't believe it." In his dilemma, he turned to Rainbow. "This runs counter to what we were saying. We agreed that Swayne wouldn't do anything about the dam until he had the land he requires. What's your idea?"

"It depends on how accurate your figures are. You told me he still needed considerable acreage. Is it possible he's picked up some property you don't know about because he hasn't filed the deeds?"

"No—no single buy would give him enough," Matt said flatly. "He'd have to make three or four deals, and we know he hasn't done that."

"Then it may be just a bluff—his way of putting more pressure on you. You know about where he plans to put the dam?"

"Sure," Buck Winters interjected. "No question about it."

"Then I'd send someone down there this afternoon," said Rip, "and look the site over. See if surveyors have lined things up—if any material has been hauled up from Buffalo Lodge."

"That makes sense," Winters declared. "I'll go down; you go with me, John. We'll be back by evenin'. If you want to have a meetin' tonight, we could hold it here."

"I wish you would," Rainbow urged. "I've had an idea rattling around in my head ever since Matt showed us where Swayne plans to cut the river. I'd like to talk it over with my partner. If he can't tear it to pieces—and I assure you gentlemen he'll try—I'll put it up to you tonight."

"Fair enough," Cameron agreed. "We'll meet here at eight o'clock."

CHAPTER SEVENTEEN

MATT AND HIS SON were absent from C Bar all afternoon, carrying word of the night's meeting at Buck Winters's Double Triangle house to the basin cowmen. This was the first time Del's services had been enlisted in that capacity. That some would question the wisdom of bringing the boys in as full partners in the fight was to be expected. Winters had not liked the idea at first, but he had been won over. It was Rainbow's opinion that no one would object too strenuously when they had had time to think it over.

Vangie came home from town to find the partners seated on the gallery. They broke off their long, and at times rather heated, discussion of Rip's plan as she drove up. Her smile was bright and questioning.

"Don't be alarmed, Miss Cameron," the tall man said laughingly, "we're not having an argument. We've just been hammering away at an idea of mine." He was sure she had heard their voices as she turned her team into the yard. "How are things in town?"

"Peaceful as can be."

"You talked to Lin?"

"For a minute. He came out as I was driving past the office. He gave me a message for you. He says he can't hold Eph Twilley longer than a day or two, unless a complaint is filed against him. Lin said you'd understand. He suggested that you get Van Hibbard to charge him with assault."

"That wouldn't stand up, Miss Cameron; Hibbard helped to tie him up. Under the law, that constitutes an assault on Twilley. Has he asked for a lawyer?"

"No. The court isn't sitting and won't be until Judge Hooker gets back on the fifteenth. Of course, there's Milo Sweet, our county prosecutor. Lin seems to think Mr. Swayne will send a lawyer up from Buffalo Lodge and get

Eph out."

"He's all wrong there, Miss Vangie," Grumpy declared with his usual positiveness. "Twilley's been found out; he's no more use to that highbinder. Swayne won't turn a finger for him."

"I agree with that," said Rip. "If you see Lin before I do, Miss Cameron, tell him I said for him to sit tight—and to see that Twilley isn't taken away from him by force."

She went on into the house. Rip turned to the little one with more than his usual soberness. "You can see how little time we have, Grump. We've got to get Lin and Twilley out of the county and spring our trap on Swayne before the judge gets back, or it's no go."

"Yeh—and I'm wonderin' if we can move fast enough. If they're lukewarm about yore proposition tonight, you better forgit it."

"I'll have to," Rainbow agreed.

The Double Triangle house was not big enough to accommodate the crowd that gathered there that evening. At Cameron's suggestion, they moved out into the yard at the rear of the house. Del and the boys who had been riding with him were there in force. As Rip had predicted, no voice was raised against their presence.

The tone of the meeting was set by Buck's report of what he and Calvin had seen at the site of the proposed dam. By now, everyone present had either seen or heard about Swayne's advertisement in the *Intelligencer*. Some regarded it as just a colossal bluff; others were either openly or secretly fearful of what it meant. What Buck had to say filled all with undisguised dismay.

"It looks like it's on the level," he declared. "We got close enough to be sure of what we were seein'. Swayne's got three or four surveyors workin'. They're drivin' stakes and doin' a lot of sightin' with their transits. Half a dozen carpenters are puttin' up some shacks. Tool sheds maybe; or they could be livin'-quarters for the foremen and bosses. While we was layin' out in the bush, takin' it all in, a freightin' outfit shows up and begins unloadin' cement.

Swayne's got gunmen there, guardin' everythin'."

Grumpy got Rip aside. "It still could be a bluff."

The tall man nodded. "That's still my opinion, Grump, but you could never make this crowd believe it. I'm not going to say anything about what I've got on my mind until they've had a chance to talk this thing over. When they start hollering for action, I'll show them how to get some."

Various suggestions for meeting the situation were made. The only ones that aroused any enthusiasm called for violence and gun smoke. Rainbow was pleased to hear Matt Cameron argue against resorting to such a course.

"I'd like to give them a dose of what they gave Nazareth last night," Matt told the crowd, "but I believe if we go down to the lower end of the basin and start throwing lead, we'll be doing exactly what Swayne wants us to do. We can't beat him with guns alone; we've got to outsmart him."

It gave Rip his cue, and he stepped up on the wagon box from which Cameron had spoken. He waited until he had the attention of the crowd. "Some of you know me; most of you don't. This much I can tell you; though my partner and I are in this fight for reasons of our own, we'll go all the way with you. I'm sure Matt is right when he says that we can't win with guns alone. If we're going to whip Swayne, we've got to trick him into making a mistake." He turned to Cameron. "Matt, I'd like to ask you a question. You're a member of the legislature; you know the law. If we could prove with indisputable evidence that Swayne is employing wanted men—killers, gunmen—to terrorize this community and whip it into line—what would happen?"

"The grant the state has given him would be revoked in short order. But we can't do it. We know the gang that raided Nazareth last night and has been making it unsafe for a man to be abroad at night are his hired men. When you talk about evidence, that's different; he sits in his office in Buffalo Lodge and pulls the strings—"

"But try to prove it!" a rancher at the rear of the crowd

growled. "He's safe down there! We can't git nothin' on the dirty skunk unless he shows his face in Nazareth Basin—and he's too smart for that!"

"Maybe we can be a little smarter than he is," Rip told the assemblage. "If we play our cards right, we can bring him into Nazareth. Before he knows what he's doing, he'll be leading the fight against us personally. That'll give us all the evidence we need to put him on the shelf."

The crowd was interested, but skeptical.

"How do you propose to do it?" Winters demanded.

"By throwing a scare into him," Rainbow replied. "Matt had us up along the river this morning and showed us where Swayne intends to let the water in. You all know the spot. Medicine River can be turned into the badlands just as easily as into the basin. There's no doubt in my mind that if we go up there and get to work making a cut to throw the river away from the basin, that he will walk into our trap."

"Yuh can't cut the river," he was told. "The law will stop us."

"I don't mean to cut the river," Rip countered. "We'll just be making a bluff at it—but we'll make it look like the real thing. We'll only have a few days; it'll have to come to a showdown before the judge gets back. And we'll have to get Lin Messenger away from Nazareth. I think that can be done."

"That's a fantastic scheme," Matt declared, with a disparaging frown. He had expected something better from Rainbow. "We wouldn't be up there twenty-four hours before Swayne heard of it—"

Rip said, "I should hope so."

"And if he's taken in by your trick and believes we actually mean to turn the river into the badlands—don't you know what he'll do?" Matt spread his hands in a hopeless gesture. "He'll get a temporary injunction. It'll stop us cold."

"How is he going to get his injunction if Hooker isn't here to grant it?"

"He'll get around that. County lines don't mean a thing

when a litigant can prove time is of the essence and that he will suffer irreparable damage if action is delayed. On that basis, he can go into court in Buffalo Lodge and get a stay—and that will be just as good as an injunction."

"Not quite," the tall man disagreed. "I'd expect him to get a stay—just as you say. But he can't send any law-enforcement officer into the basin to serve us with it. The only officer who can serve it is Lin Messenger—and as I said, I think we can get Lin out of the way."

The crowd was listening intently, anxious not to miss a word.

"I can shoot that argument full of holes," Matt persisted, with growing impatience. "A court order of that kind can be served by anyone. Swayne can serve it himself."

"Of course he can," the tall man agreed. Unwittingly, Cameron was feeding him the very argument he wanted. "And that's what Swayne will do when he realizes it's the only move he has left. Having run into one delay after another, he'll be desperate by then. Remember, we'll be working day and night—drilling and blasting. He'll have to do something in a hurry. I know his kind. My partner and I have fought them for years. Swayne will throw caution to the winds and show up in Nazareth, surrounded with bodyguards and his lawyers. And he'll have a hatful of John Doe summonses. We'll see to it that he has some difficulty serving them. We won't molest the man; that would ruin everything; but we can make it uncomfortable for him."

Frank Warren raised his voice. "I know Swayne! He won't take much of that!"

"I'm sure he won't, Frank. He'll bring his gun slingers down from Silver Gulch and join up with them. That'll be his undoing."

Cameron heard the muttered approval on all sides. He was not ready to give Rainbow's plan his approval. "Sounds like it's all adding up to a big gun fight showdown," he declared soberly. "I don't like that part of it."

"There'll be a fight," Rainbow admitted. "I don't believe that can be avoided. But it won't be just a case of trading lead—not if our timing is right. A lot is going to depend on what Messenger does. If he'll play it our way, we'll wind this thing up for keeps."

Buck Winters pushed forward a step or two. "That's the second or third time you've mentioned Lin. You said somethin' about gittin' him out of the county. How you figurin' to do that?"

The tall man smiled soberly. "We'll have to convince him that Twilley will be safer if he's removed from Nazareth and lodged in the Yellowstone County jail, in Billings. If all of you will ride into town, when the meeting breaks up, and surround the jail and put on a noisy demonstration, I think Lin can be persuaded to take Twilley to Billings. After he goes, we'll have to move fast; he won't be away more than three or four days."

"What makes you think he'll be gone that long?" Matt was quick to ask. "If you pull the wool over his eyes, you can't be sure when he'll come busting back—"

"Matt, I don't intend to pull the wool over Lin's eyes. He won't break his oath—I wouldn't ask him to—but I know he'll lean over backward to help us. If he's tipped off that we want him to stay away, he'll stay away."

It won the chorused agreement of the crowd. Rainbow was applauded as he stepped down. A dozen men or more began speaking at once, each trying to make himself heard over the others.

Grumpy edged up to the tall man. "You made a hit with 'em, Rip. I don't know about Cameron—he seems to be on the fence—but the others are with you to a man."

"He's mulling it over," Rainbow returned quietly, glancing at Matt. "I didn't expect him to get excited about it; he's a cautious man."

A few moments later, Matt stepped up on the wagon box again and raised his hands to get the attention of the crowd. It was several minutes before he could proceed.

"I came to this meeting without having any previous knowledge of what our friend here was going to say," he began, indicating Rip with a wave of the hand. "I can assure you he is a man of experience and proven judgment. I knew he was going to advise us what to do. Maybe I got my hopes up too high, thinking he could suggest an easy way out of this trouble. I'm afraid there isn't any easy way. But he's shown us a course of action we can take. A few minutes ago I said it was fantastic; and so it is. That's not to condemn it; the very fact that it is so fantastic gives me the feeling that it may succeed. It may not. But Swayne's latest move seems to indicate that the crisis is here; so unless someone has something better to suggest, I'll go through with this scheme of pretending to turn the river, if you will."

The crowd's excited response left no doubt as to how it felt.

"We've got the dynamite we'll need," Matt continued, "and many of us know how to drive a drill. We can arrange as to who will work through the day and who will be on the job by night. If it's agreeable to all, be at my place tomorrow morning at seven. And bring your rifles with you. There's no use pretending we won't have to face a lot of sniping from the scrub timber on the lower hills."

"If I can make a suggestion," Rip called out, "we'll plant a number of men on that hillside. It'll make Swayne realize we mean business and don't intend to be run off the riverbank. Turning back his gunmen will be a tough job, but if you'll give my partner and me half a dozen men who don't mind some gun smoke, we'll dig in up there."

A score volunteered. Rainbow left it to Matt to pick the best men. When that had been done, there remained the more difficult job of devising a system of rotation for the men who were to work at the cut. That was finally accomplished to the satisfaction of all.

"What about grub?" Warren inquired.

"Let each man bring his own," said Matt. "I'll arrange to have plenty of coffee up there; the rest will be up to you."

It lacked a few minutes of eleven o'clock when half a hundred men raced into Nazareth and quickly surrounded the jail. Messenger was caught alone. During the day, small groups of townspeople had gathered out in front several times and expressed their desire to get their hands on Twilley. He had not regarded it seriously, and when ten o'clock passed peacefully, he told Thompson to go home.

Save for the fact that the milling crowd punctuated its demands that he produce the prisoner by firing half a hundred shots into the air, the scene was a repetition of what had taken place the previous evening. By arrangement, Matt Cameron arrived tardily and pleaded with the men to disperse. After much hooting and jeering, they withdrew.

Lin watched it all through the barred wicket in the door, recognizing most of the participants. The partners were conspicuous by their absence.

The latter were waiting at the edge of town. When the Camerons came along, they joined them and rode back to C Bar.

"I don't know whether we fooled Lin or not," said Matt. He wasn't happy about it. "It looked like the real thing."

"Don't distress yourself about it," Rainbow told him. "I'll ride into town in the morning and have a talk with him. Grumpy will go with the other men, and I'll be along by noon."

He was back in Nazareth before eight and went at once to Johnny Wong's for breakfast. Mei-lang had not come down as yet. Cheng saw him and informed her that he had come in. She took her place at the desk without noticing him, and after two other diners had left, Rainbow informed her of what he expected the next four or five days to bring.

"You sound very confident this morning, Rainbow," she told him.

"Not overconfident, I hope. You can plan these things carefully, but they never work out quite as one hopes. There isn't any doubt in my mind that we'll bring Swayne to Nazareth. This is the only restaurant in town, so he'll eat here. If you can make him and the men he'll have with him believe you neither understand nor speak English, they may talk freely enough to let something slip. If so, and you feel it's important, send Cheng to the Cameron ranch with the message."

Her eyes were wistful as she gazed at him. "You say nothing about it, but there's danger in this for you—great danger. I've said it so many times—I can only say it again—be careful, darling! It's bad enough not to see you for months at a time; but that's quite different from the loneliness that would come to me if anything happened to you."

He smiled at her fondly. "I remember a night a few years ago when a beautiful and gracious lady gave me a ring. She said it was a talisman—that it would bring me luck. Her name was Mei-lang. The ring has never failed me. I know it never will."

A ranch mother and her two children approached the door and he had to say a hasty farewell. He paid his check and went on up the street. Lin Messenger was at his desk, with the door standing open.

"I had company last night," Lin said, grinning. "I didn't see anything of you or Grumpy. What kept you away?"

"Nobody sent us an invitation," Rainbow answered, in the same bantering tone. "You're gay, for so early in the morning, Lin. What's so amusing?"

He surmised that he could supply the answer.

Messenger laughed. "That business last night, Rip. I saw Henry Colfax out there, whooping it up with the others. That was the tip-off that it wasn't on the level. Old Henry's a Quaker—a religious man—he wouldn't take a hand in a necktie party."

The tall man met it with a poker face. "You could be wrong. But whether you are or not, you've got all the excuse you need for guarding the safety of your prisoner by removing him from this county—to Billings, for instance."

Messenger brought his chair down on all four legs, with a bang. "So that's it!" he said tensely, leaning across the desk.

"That's it," Rip replied. "I arranged that party last night. I wouldn't ask you to do a thing that would violate your oath of office, Lin. But you're a Nazareth man; you know what the Camerons and all these other folks are up against. They're being handed a rotten, crooked deal. If you'll get on the noon stage with Twilley, you can catch a train out of Buffalo Lodge tomorrow for Billings. Stay away three or four days, Lin. I wouldn't ask it if I wasn't convinced that I've found a way to turn the tables on Swayne. You'll be back in time to take charge."

Messenger swung around in his chair and stared through the open door in deep abstraction. Finally, he said, "I'm not going to ask you what your plans are; but you're going to break the law, of course."

"Only technically, Lin—"

"And Vangie—is she going to be in any danger?"

"None whatsoever. I guarantee it."

"All right!" Lin jerked out with sudden decision. "When the noon stage pulls out, I'll be on it with Twilley!"

CHAPTER EIGHTEEN

AT MESSENGER'S REQUEST, Rip stopped at C Bar on his way up the basin to deliver a message to Vangie. Her surprise, on reading the letter, led the tall man to believe that her father had not taken her into confidence regarding the plans now afoot.

"Of course you know why he is leaving for Billings," she said when she had read the letter. "I can't understand why he's to be gone so long."

"I suppose he has business to transact," Rainbow replied with deliberate evasiveness. "I must ask you to stay close to home while he's away, Miss Cameron. If you have to go to town, don't go alone. This trouble with Swayne is coming to a head in the next few days. If we have a little luck, we may have a showdown soon after Lin gets back. In the meantime, don't forget that your father is a leading figure in this fight. It may sound farfetched to say that Swayne might try to get at him by harming you; but it's something to consider."

Though some of the color left her cheeks, Vangie managed a smile. "I'll do as you say, Mr. Ripley; but I can't help thinking it's preposterous to think that any harm could come to me—"

"When men are playing for big stakes, nothing is preposterous, Miss Cameron," the tall man told her.

He and Grumpy still had some of their personal belongings in the old wagon. He went on to the barn and got his rifle, cartridges, and binoculars. A few minutes later, he was on his way up the basin.

While he was still several miles from the scene of operations on the river, the air was suddenly filled with a low, grumbling reverberation that could have been produced only by the exploding of dynamite or giant powder. Recognizing it for what it was, Rip smiled with satisfaction. Obviously Matt and his men were not losing any time.

Though he was not aware of it, the blast he heard was the third that had been discharged. Under Matt's direction, the splintered rock being dislodged was piled up to form a circular parapet, behind which the basin men might reasonably hope to withstand attack, no matter from which direction it came.

Rainbow expressed his approval. "Piling this stuff up means that you can't be caught out here in the open. But it's that hillside we've got to worry about. When they find they can't get through that way, there's no telling what they may try. We may have to pull down your bridge, Matt."

"No great objection to that," the owner of C Bar said. "If we win this fight, I can build a new bridge. What about Lin?"

"He left on the noon stage with Twilley. He won't be back for a few days. But we didn't fool him last night."

"I'm glad we didn't," said Matt. "I know what I'd get from my daughter if she thought I'd had a hand in putting something over on him. He agreed to stay away, eh?"

Rip smiled thinly. "He won't be back for a few days—let's put it that way— You're making this job look like the real thing."

"Huh!" the owner of C Bar grunted. "I'm glad it ain't the real thing! With the tools we've got, we'd be here all summer. Rotten quartz and granite on top, but we've hit solid base rock already. Drills have to be sharpened every few minutes."

After talking with John Calvin and the other ranchers, Rip joined Grumpy and his party in the brush and scrub-covered foothill. They had hidden their horses and deployed themselves to advantage.

The tall man was glad to see that Buck Winters and Frank Warren were among the half-dozen men with Grumpy. They struck him as being thoroughly dependable. The others were strangers to him.

"Sounds like we're all set," Buck declared, when Rip had given them his news about Messenger and Twilley. "As long as we're goin' to stick it out here till this thing breaks one way or the other, Ripley, is there any reason why we shouldn't get acquainted?"

"None at all, Buck. The time for holding anything back has passed."

They shook hands all around. It did not surprise the partners to learn that their identity had been a loosely kept secret at best.

"Buck and me made a little scout through here before we settled on this spot," Grumpy explained. "The cover is good; and the ground dips away purty sharp in front of us. I figger we can stick here as long as necessary—and we ain't more'n five, six hundred yards from the boys workin' on the river."

"It's all right," Rip assured him. "This blasting will be heard miles away. If Swayne's got anyone drifting through these hills, they'll investigate. We're likely to see one or two of them during the afternoon. They won't try to get through; they'll be satisfied to get an eyeful of what's going on. Remember this—our game, for the present, is not to let them know we're up here. They may get close enough to give our nerves a workout. We'll either be equal to it or we'll ruin everything."

They spread out and concealed themselves. No more than an hour had passed when they saw a rider picking his way through the scrub. He came on and on until he was only seventy-five yards away. When he pulled up, they caught his sharp grunt of surprise as he saw what was being done on the river. Wheeling his horse, he dashed back the way he had come.

The afternoon dragged on, and just before five o'clock, the snapping of brush, higher up the slope, cried a warning. Buck Winters caught the first glimpse of them. "Three of 'em this time!" he called quietly to the partners.

The latter located the intruders a moment later, and got a surprise. One of the three was the one they had seen earlier in the afternoon; the second was a smallish man in brown corduroys whose appearance was not that of a gunman; the third man was Ben Slade.

They reached the spot where the first man had stopped

and surveyed the activity below. What was being done there left nothing to the imagination. The man in the corduroys (the partners wondered if he was Noah Swayne) kept his temper; Slade cursed violently. The two of them argued about something. Both seemed satisfied with the decision they reached. They remained only a few minutes. With Slade leading the way, they went back up the slope and when they reached a trail, put spurs to their broncs.

Rainbow waited a quarter of an hour, making sure an attack wasn't imminent, before he and Grumpy got up and called Buck and the others around them.

"Was that Swayne in the corduroys?" the little one inquired at once.

"No, Ron Huggins, Swayne's right-hand man," Buck answered. "He sticks purty close to the office in Buffalo Lodge, as a rule. What do you figger they was arguin' about, boys?"

"I think I can be a hundred-percent sure about that," said Rainbow. "Huggins wanted to put it up to the boss; Slade was all for bringing up his gang and making a gun fight of it. If I read it correctly, we'll get it both ways now; Huggins will lose no time getting to Swayne, who'll start the legal wheels turning; Slade will be back with his gun slicks—either tonight or in the morning."

"This man you call Slade—you speak as if you know him," Warren remarked.

"We know him," Grumpy growled. "We came a long ways to nab him." He glanced up inquiringly at Rip. "They're shore to be comin' at us. How do we handle it? Do we start the ball rollin', or do we wait for them to open up?"

"This hillside belongs to Matt Cameron; we're here with his consent," the tall man answered with great soberness. "When we hear them coming, we'll fire a warning volley; but that will be all until we're actually attacked. We want them to be the aggressors." He looked about, making sure that all were listening and understood what he was saying. "When we have been given sufficient provocation, we have the legal right to defend this land and ourselves. Is that clear to everybody?"

There was a unanimous nodding of heads.

"No question but what we'll be throwing away an advantage in letting them bring the fight to us," Rip continued. "It'll be worth it if we can make it impossible for Swayne to claim that we were not acting in self-defense."

He walked down to the cut and told Matt what had occurred. "I can give you more men for tonight," the latter offered.

"No, I have enough," said Rainbow. "We may not hear from them till morning. But whatever you do, Matt, don't try to send help to us, no matter how you think the fight is going. If you'll stay put, we'll know who we're shooting at if we hear anybody moving around behind us."

Night fell, and Rip stretched out behind a boulder, his rifle beside him. Eight feet away, Grumpy made himself comfortable in the lee of a shallow outcropping. What conversation they had was restricted to whispers. Hours passed and the stillness of the grave shrouded the hillside.

"After midnight," Grumpy whispered. "If they was comin' tonight, they'd be here by now."

The little man's prediction proved correct, and dawn was in the air when they heard a telltale snapping of brush. Rip gave the signal and a warning volley tore through the scrub, the slugs clipping off twigs and leaves.

After the echoes died away, the morning was still again. Too still for Rainbow, who ordered another volley. It brought no immediate answer, but Buck soon passed word to him that Swayne's men had been seen slipping down into the dip in the hillside, thirty yards in front of them.

It was growing lighter by the second, but Rip could feel rather than see the tension gripping Buck and the others. "Don't get overanxious," he cautioned. "Let them open up."

The words were barely out of his mouth when a dozen searching shots pinged off the rocks behind which he and his party were lying. He got a flash of half a dozen men, only their heads showing, peering over the lip of the depression. "Okay!" he cried. "Let 'em have it!"

The shooting swelled in a furious crescendo and for ten minutes or more was continuous. The attackers were still in the dip, however, and either unable or unwilling to risk a further advance.

How the other side had fared, there was no telling, but among the basin men, only one had been struck and he by a ricocheting slug that burned a fiery streak across his left arm.

"Is Slade with him, Grump?" Rainbow queried.

"Yeh, I saw him! We can't make no exception of him, Rip—"

"Not if we get a shot at him."

After a brief interval the attack was renewed. One man managed to get out of the dip. He rolled up behind the safety of a rock, but after firing a shot or two, and seeing that he alone had made it, he plunged back out of sight.

Slade ordered a third charge. Its feebleness hinted that it was only a feint. Proof of it came several minutes later when he and five others were detected trying to get around below the defenders. Warren knocked down one of them. Grumpy and Buck joined Warren; between them, they ended that threat.

For the next half hour, only an occasional shot was fired. Grumpy raised himself up on an elbow and caught Rainbow's attention. "They're pullin' back," he muttered. "Those last three or four shots came from the same gun."

The tall man nodded. "I thought I heard them going through the brush. We'll stay where we are; this may be a trick."

By seven o'clock, he felt it safe to reconnoiter the slope. He was gone some time. When he came back it was with word that they had the hill to themselves.

"They're carrying some wounded men with them," he said. "Bloodstains on the grass in three or four places."

"How about that bird I knocked down?" Warren asked. "I thought I finished him."

"If so, they picked him up. We gave them a licking; I don't believe they'll be back. Reckon we can light a fire and boil some coffee."

He had a look at Vic Southard's wounded arm and advised him to see a doctor.

"It don't amount to nothin'," Southard protested. "I'll go down to the river and wash it out and forgit it." He grinned approvingly at the tall man. "You called every turn they've made so far, Ripley. I'm damned if a man don't have to go all the way with you now."

A smile lifted the corners of Rainbow's mouth. "It's apt to be a rocky road, Vic."

The day passed without further incident. Down at the cut, Matt had established a routine that did away with the confusion of the previous day. Young Del and several other boys had been called on to bring up food and news from C Bar and the other ranches in the upper basin. There was no news from Nazareth.

With evening coming on again, Rainbow announced that he was going to town. "Swayne's had time enough to make some sort of move," he told Grumpy. "I won't be gone long. When I get back to the cut, I'll signal you before I come up."

"I don't see why it's necessary for you to go," the little one grumbled. "What about Mei-lang? If anythin' important had happened, she'd have got word to you."

"I'm sure of that, Grump. I don't believe anything really important has happened; it's too soon. But if Swayne's done anything, I want to know what it is. If possible, I want to keep one jump ahead of him."

He slipped into Nazareth without attracting any attention. The town still bore most of the marks of the raid. He found the restaurant closed for the night. Wong sat at the desk, figuring out his accounts with the aid of an abacus. Rip tapped on the window. Johnny admitted him and showed him upstairs to the family living-room.

It wasn't necessary to call Mei-lang. Having recognized his voice on the stairs, she was waiting for him.

"Is there something wrong, Rainbow?" she asked at once, and with more surprise than she usually exhibited.

"No," he assured her. "We had some trouble this morning, but it went our way."

She was relieved to see that he had not been wounded. "And Grumpy?" she queried.

"Neither one of us got so much as a scratch."

Cheng came to the door and greeted him. They exchanged a few words. When Mei-lang nodded, he and Wong withdrew.

Rainbow sat down beside her. Her nearness, the faint perfume of her hair, overwhelmed him. He raised her hand, with its long, exquisite fingers to his lips. The next moment she was in his arms. He was a long time releasing her.

With the poise that never deserted her, she sat back, her firm young breasts rising and falling in her smothered agitation. "You—make me forget why we are here, Rainbow. I know why you came to town—"

"Swayne," he said, and she nodded, understanding fully.

"I was writing you a note that I was going to have Cheng take up to the Cameron ranch in the morning. Two of his lawyers were in Nazareth this morning. They went to the courthouse at once. When they learned the judge was away, they went to the sheriff's office. On being informed that Mr. Messenger had gone to Billings and wasn't expected back for several days, they were furious, I understand. They returned to Buffalo Lodge on the noon stage."

Rip was delighted with the news. "That's exactly what I wanted to know, Mei-lang! If I've got things figured out correctly, we'll see Swayne himself next."

"Tomorrow?"

"Tomorrow or the next day—depending on how long it takes him to recruit some bodyguards. He won't come up alone. Were those lawyers in the restaurant?"

"They came in for sandwiches, just before the stage left." Mei-lang smiled amusedly. "They tried to get me to hurry their order; but I couldn't understand their English and they threw up their hands at my Chinese. They talked freely. I overheard one of them say Swayne would have to serve his own papers. The other expressed his doubts about anyone being able to do it."

"Well, we'll make it difficult," said Rainbow. His mood was confident, even gay.

After spending half an hour with her, he got up to leave. Though he was anxious to be back, she refused to let him go until he had had some refreshments. She went to the door and spoke to Wong. The latter appeared soon after with a tray on which were tea, cakes, and Chinese preserved fruits.

The little repast provided a pleasant interlude, and over the teacups, something ran between them that was precious and intimate.

At his suggestion, she let him out by the back door. After going down the alley a few yards, he cut back to the street, found his horse, and was soon on his way up the basin.

The night was bright with moonlight. Lulled to carelessness by his thoughts of Mei-lang, he followed the C Bar fence until he was a mile below the spot where the men were working. In the distance, their flickering fire cast an orange glow that seemed to intensify the indigo blackness beneath a tall clump of sagebrush. Approaching it, his dreaming was rudely shattered by a sharp command to throw up his hands.

He had seldom been caught at such a disadvantage. But as he was raising his hands, a burst of laughter stopped him, and Van Hibbard stepped into view.

"It's so bright I recognized you some distance back," young Hibbard told him. "I didn't figure we'd catch you napping, Rip."

The tall man didn't attempt to conceal his chagrin. "What are you doing, lying out here?" he asked.

"I ain't alone," said Van. "Cameron's got three or four of us posted along the river."

"Not a bad idea," Rainbow observed. "I'll try to be ready, the next time I'm stopped."

He was stopped three times before he reached the log bridge. Before saying anything to Matt about what he had learned in town, he complimented him for his astuteness in placing the boys along the river.

"I had to find something for them to do," Matt declared. "They've been pestering me to death— What's the news, Rip?"

Ten men were there to work through the night. They gathered around him to hear what he had to say. They found what little he had to tell them as encouraging as he did.

"The next forty-eight hours could tell the story," he went on. "There is not the slightest doubt in my mind but what we'll see Swayne in person. When he marches up here to serve his papers, he'll be smart enough to come unarmed. We'll have to hold him off until he is so exasperated he'll go berserk. We can't use our guns on him. If we do—all this has been for nothing. I can suggest one or two things; no doubt you can, too."

Some of the ideas advanced were so absurd that they were dismissed almost as soon as uttered; others were discussed at great length. Out of the many suggestions made, they settled on several that were practical and calculated to succeed. Having got that far, they spent an hour working out the details of how the maneuvers were to be executed.

"Ripley's idea of using the cattle is the best one," Matt commented. "We'll use it first and be ready with Calvin's trick next."

"If we turn Swayne back once or twice, that'll be enough," said Rainbow. "I'll bid you gentlemen good night."

Plucking a burning faggot out of the fire and holding it aloft, he crossed the bridge and went up the slope.

CHAPTER NINETEEN

THE BLASTING CONTINUED throughout the night, a charge being touched off every two hours, though very little drilling was being done. The cut was deep enough by now so that no one in the hills, even with the aid of powerful glasses, could see what was being done. The numerous explosions were intended to convey the impression of feverish activity to any listening ear.

Rainbow expressed no surprise over Slade's failure to put in another appearance with his gunmen.

"They're holding off because Swayne has taken charge," he commented, over his morning coffee as he and the others gathered about the fire, getting the night chill out of their bones.

"If that's the explanation," said Buck, "we'll be seein' him today, not tomorrow."

"I'd say that was a reasonable conclusion," Rip agreed.

"If that's the case, Rip, Matt ought to be holding every man on the river. We been stickin' it out; there's no reason why they can't."

"By grab, that's the way it strikes me," Grumpy declared testily. He got up and walked over to an opening in the brush that permitted a view of the cut. "The day shift is jest comin' on," he announced. "You better git down there, Rip, and have a talk with Matt. We can use three or four more men up here."

The tall man went down the slope at once. He was seen from below, and his signal to the men who were leaving held them back. As he walked across the bridge, he examined it with fresh interest. It was a crude affair constructed by laying two long stringers across the stream and nailing on them a surface of planks. Its only purpose was to permit C Bar to bring timber down to the ranch.

Matt was waiting for him. "I saw you looking the bridge over. Do you think we better pull it down?"

"No, we may need it. But we can rip up the planks and pile them up on this side. That'll leave just the stringers. If you fetch up some grease, you can plaster them with it. That'll make it impossible for anybody to get across. I've been thinking over the suggestion Calvin made last night about blocking the county bridge east of town. We better do it while we have time. Pile up some wagons there and chain and padlock them together. That'll make it next to impossible for Swayne to reach you with his papers."

The night before, they had explained to him that Medicine River could be forded in several places below Nazareth, but when a man got across, he could not proceed far before a series of sharp cliffs would stop him. Up above, the river buried itself in an impassable canyon.

"All right," Matt agreed, "it'll be done. You sound as though you figured Swayne would be showing up today."

"Everything points to it," Rip said. "That's why I stopped you men from leaving. If this is the showdown, we're all going to be needed. Counting the boys, there'll be about forty of us in all. I can use four or five more men on the hill."

No one demurred when Cameron asked them to stay.

"We can grab a little sleep right here," said one.

Matt selected five men to go up with Rainbow.

"Take your broncs up with you," the tall man told them. "When we get across, Matt, pull up the planks."

Cameron assured him it would be done. "We'll begin on the other side and smear the stringers with tallow as we work back." He laughed grimly at the thought of a man trying to negotiate the greased stringers. "If you look down in the basin, you'll see my crew beginning to bunch the cows. They'll have about five hundred head altogether. That ought to be enough."

"It'll be more than enough," said Rainbow.

Mei-lang witnessed the arrival of the morning stage. Usually it carried only two or three passengers. This morning, it was so crowded that two men rode on top with the driver. Before the stage had time to discharge its passengers, word ran up the street that Noah Swayne was in Nazareth.

He was accompanied by the two lawyers who had been there the previous day, Ron Huggins, his chief lieutenant, and five tough-looking characters who were correctly catalogued as his bodyguards.

The whole party proceeded to the town's only livery and ordered Lester Moss, the proprietor, to supply them with saddle horses. Lester had the horses to rent, but he refused to let Swayne have them. One of the guards knocked him down and gave him a beating that brought him to terms.

Mei-lang and Cheng watched the party jog past the restaurant and head up the basin. The air of authority he gave himself made it easy for them to identify the big, florid-faced man, wearing riding-breeches, as Noah Swayne. If he or his companions were armed, they had no guns showing.

Cheng Bow wanted to leave for the Cameron ranch immediately. Mei-lang said no.

"You'd be too late, Cheng; they'll be seen by the men on the river before we could get word to them."

Rainbow had been sweeping the basin with his binoculars for some time when he sighted the party. He handed the glasses to Buck and the latter instantly confirmed that it was Swayne and his hirelings. Word was sent down to the men at the cut, and they responded by setting off another blast.

The stage was all set now, and the basin men and the partners waited eagerly for the first act, in which they expected to play no part, to begin.

Swayne and his little cavalcade came on unopposed until they were less than half a mile from the cut. Off to their left, the C Bar herd had begun milling. It could not have gone unnoticed by Swayne's party, but they could hardly have surmised what was to follow, for suddenly Matt's crew had the cows running. Even then, the wild hallooing and slapping of coiled ropes could have been an honest attempt by Matt's punchers to turn the cattle. But it wasn't; the stampede was deliberate and nicely timed.

Straight for Swayne and his cohorts the cows drove, tails up and heads down, their mad bellowing being the best evidence in the world that they were really getting "spooked up," as the old saying has it.

With that sea of flashing horns bearing down on them, there was nothing for Swayne's forces to do but turn tail and run. The C Bar crew chased them for two miles.

The watchers enjoyed their first good laugh in days.

"They won't stop till they hit my fence!" Buck chortled. "The way them skunks lit out was somethin' to see!"

The cows were lost to view beyond the undulations of the basin floor. The crew got them to circling and quieted down.

An hour later, Swayne made a second attempt to get up to the cut and serve his papers. He followed the C Bar fence this time and moved cautiously. But he and his men were seen, and again the cows were driven at them. They didn't wait. Turning tail, they fled in disorder, with each man looking out for himself.

"They won't try that again," Rip predicted. "I hope that bridge east of town is blocked. They'll certainly attempt to work up the river next."

Swayne tried the county bridge and found he couldn't get through. He was beside himself by now and every fresh blast that reverberated across the basin further infuriated him. Months ago, before divulging his plans, he had acquainted himself with the country. Reckless by now, he decided to try getting up the river by going through C Bar, dangerous as that might be. But there was no one there except Vangie and her mother. Late in the afternoon they saw him and his men stealing along between the house and the bank.

Half a mile above the house, they had no choice but to move out into the open, with not even brush to screen them. They rode out boldly, hoping to impress the basin men with their authority, Swayne riding in the lead.

At the cut, work ceased and the men flattened down behind the rock parapet they had erected. Eyes were glued to the interstices in the rocks. Up on the slope, the partners and the men with them watched just as closely.

When Swayne and his adherents got close enough to the old log bridge to see that it had been stripped and only the skeleton remained, they stopped for a consultation. After a few minutes, Swayne advanced by himself until he was opposite the men concealed in the cut. The fact that not a shot had been fired up to now, apparently convinced him that he was in no danger of being cut down.

"You know why I'm here!" he yelled, waving a sheaf of papers, his angry voice rising above the roar of the river. "Everyone of you is in contempt of court! You'll accept service of these papers or you'll go to jail!"

"Come on over and serve yore papers!" a raucous voice taunted.

"By God, I will!" Swayne bellowed, his heavy face black with rage.

Balancing himself he started across one of the greased stringers. He took only a step or two, however, when his legs went flying out from under him and he plunged headlong into the rushing river, eighteen feet below. He was instantly swept away and carried several hundred yards downstream before he was fished out, dripping and sputtering.

There was no holding back the laughter of the basin men. Even Rainbow could not repress a chuckle.

"We did better than I had any reason to believe we would," he said, watching Swayne and his party moving down the basin. "He's through for the day; he'll play a different tune tomorrow."

Buck caught an uneasy note in the tall man's tone. "What's eatin' you? You planned it that way."

"I know," Rip acknowledged. "We've got Swayne in the frame of mind we wanted. I'm sure he'll tear into us tomorrow with every man he can muster."

"So what?" Buck demanded cockily. "We'll round up that gang before we're through— Is there any doubt of it in your mind?"

"No," the tall man muttered soberly. "I was just thinking of the price we may have to pay."

Nazareth had a hotel of sorts, presently called the Star. Over the years it had had many names and many owners. It was a shabby, uncomfortable place, offering lodgings without meals. Swayne and his party found accommodations there, the proprietor being afraid to refuse to take them in, in view of the treatment Lester Moss had received at the livery barn.

The main street presented a deserted appearance; but the men of Nazareth were keyed up to such a pitch that it needed only a minor incident to touch off a conflagration. From a hundred vantage points, hostile eyes watched Swayne and his party step out of the hotel and file into Johnny Wong's restaurant.

The establishment's three or four regular diners had remained away this evening, knowing as Mei-lang and Johnny did that Swayne's crowd would be in. Johnny was understandably nervous and alarmed. He would have closed his place, but Mei-lang wouldn't hear of it. When the visitors came in, she was seated at the desk, her face a stony mask.

Swayne looked her over with a lustful eye, after he was seated. "Say, sister," he said with coarse familiarity, "can't you get off that stool and take our order?"

"Noah, you're wasting your time, talking to her," Dan Whitlock, the older of two lawyers, said laughingly. "We were in here yesterday. All we could get out of her was a lot of Chink gibberish. She can't understand a word of English."

"She ain't bad-looking," Swayne commented. "Here's the boss, I guess. We'll see what he can dish up for us."

They talked freely as they waited to be served.

One of the lawyers said, "Where's Huggins? He didn't come in with us."

"He won't be in," was Swayne's gruff response. "I sent him up to get Slade and the boys. These people want hell, and I'm going to give it to them. I'll push 'em off the river before daylight."

"Noah, you're making a mistake," Whitlock said flatly. "Pat and I have begged you not to show your hand. If these basin stockmen get any evidence that you are directing this violence, you're licked."

Pat Grady, the other lawyer, was equally exercised.

"I've listened to you long enough!" Swayne growled. "If I'd played it my way and got tough with these people weeks ago, I wouldn't be in a jam right now. If they turn the river, I'll be licked a damned sight quicker than turning Slade loose on 'em."

"What have you ordered him to do?" Whitlock demanded.

"Burn every stack of hay and barn in the basin! If that don't bring these bastards to terms, I'll burn their houses!"

Mei-lang was catching every word of it. A glance in back convinced her that Cheng was hearing it, too.

The lawyers shook their heads, and after Whitlock had whispered something in Grady's ear, he said, "You're going too far for me, Noah. I don't know how Pat feels about it, but as far as I'm concerned, you'll have to get yourself a new attorney. If I can hire someone to drive me down to the Lodge, I'll leave this evening."

"I'll go with you, Dan," Grady announced. "I've turned some sharp corners for you, Swayne; but I knew when you had that liveryman beaten up this morning, that I had enough."

"Go ahead!" Swayne cried defiantly, shaking with fury. "I ain't keeping you! You birds will miss the fat fees I been paying for your advice!"

They wrangled bitterly as they ate. When they finished, Swayne paid the bill and marched out with his guards, leaving Whitlock and Grady to get back to Buffalo Lodge any way they pleased.

They were no sooner gone than Mei-lang hastened back to the kitchen and ordered Cheng to get two saddled horses at once.

"Two?" was his surprised query.

"Yes, I am going with you— And inquire the way to the Cameron ranch!"

She ran upstairs and got into a blouse, breeches, and riding-boots. After she had waited impatiently for a quarter of an hour, Cheng appeared in the alley with the horses. Using the alley, they reached the edge of town and put spurs to their mounts.

They had not gone half a mile, when the sky began to show a crimson tinge across the basin. It mushroomed so quickly that there seemed no doubt but what a haystack had been fired. A second blaze was noticeable a few minutes later. Mei-lang responded by calling on her horse for greater speed.

Though this was the first time either she or Cheng had been in the upper basin, they found the C Bar house without difficulty. Reb Powers, Cameron's foreman, stepped out of the shadows and confronted them as they drew up at the porch. He was usually a taciturn individual, but he could not repress a start of surprise on discovering that the visitors were Chinese.

"I have a very urgent message for Mr. Ripley," Mei-lang told him. "Could you take me to him at once?"

Vangie heard their voices and hurried out. She, too, was surprised at seeing Mei-lang. "You are the young woman I've seen in Wong's, aren't you?"

"Yes," Mei-lang said, "but I'm not what I've pretended to be. Cheng and I came to Nazareth to work with Mr. Ripley and Mr. Gibbs. I just told this gentleman that I have a most urgent message for them. Swayne has sent his gunmen into the basin to burn every barn and haystack they find. Tomorrow, he intends to burn your houses."

"I figgered that's what them fires was!" Reb declared bitterly. "If it's all right with you, Vangie, I'll take these folks up the river— I'll be right back."

"Hurry, Reb! We'll be all right here."

Matt had the boys posted along the river again. Del was the first one Reb encountered. He turned Mei-lang and Cheng over to him and raced back to the house.

Loose planks had been laid across the dismantled bridge.

"We'll have to leave the horses here and go across on foot," Del said.

To Matt and his men, Mei-lang had to explain again who she was and why she was there. They had seen the fires down the basin and surmised what they were. Her news so enraged them that she had difficulty finishing.

Matt had the campfire built up. By its light and after much hallooing, he got the attention of the men on the hillside. It brought Rainbow hurrying down. For his benefit, Mei-lang repeated her story in detail.

"You and Cheng heard him say all that?" he demanded soberly.

"Every word, Rainbow."

The tall man turned to Cameron. "Matt, isn't that enough to finish Swayne with the state?"

"It is—if they'll make affidavits to that effect. But that won't stop what's going on in the basin right now."

"We'll do something about that directly," was the tall man's tight-lipped response. "Mei-lang—I want you and Cheng to go back to the C Bar house and remain there until I send for you. The Camerons will take you in, I'm sure."

"Gladly," Matt assured her. "After what you've done for us, the best we have isn't good enough."

Del left with them at once. They had no sooner gone than Rip said, "Some of you are going to lose your barns and your hay. That can't be helped; but if we move fast enough, we can round up that gang and finish them off for keeps." His glance took in Matt and the rest of the men. "You can either play this my way, or I'll play it your way. What do you say?"

"Your way is good enough for us!" Matt declared without hesitation. The others were equally positive.

"Very well," Rainbow told them. "There's no point in staying here at the cut, and no need to keep anyone up on the slope. Get them down right away, with their horses. While we're waiting, put some more planks on the bridge so you can walk your animals over. The minutes are important now!"

CHAPTER TWENTY

Half a dozen fires were burning in the basin before Grumpy and the others got down from the slope. Each fresh blaze pinpointed the position of the invading gunmen with dreadful accuracy.

"There goes my barn!" John Calvin groaned. "Built only a year ago!"

"Don't take it too hard, John," Matt advised. "Our barns and the hay won't mean anything to us if we're driven out. We're fighting for the right to stay here; don't forget that."

Rainbow called Buck Winters up to him. "Buck, you're acquainted with the trail that comes down from Silver Gulch. Grumpy will come with me; I want you to take the rest of your party and skirt up along the western edge of the basin until you're in position to block the trail and make it impossible for that gang to get out of the basin on that side. We'll go up along the river and get them in between us. You'll know when we start pushing them toward you. If they don't give up, shoot them down. Have no mercy on them. Have you got that straight, now?"

"I'll say I have!" Buck rapped. "Just give us thirty—forty minutes to get set!" Calling to his men, he struck out for the floor of the basin.

"Come on!" Rip cried. "We can be moving, too!"

As they picked their way down the river, he informed Grumpy of the news Mei-lang had brought.

"Huh!" the little one grunted disappointedly. "I figgered Swayne was with 'em."

"Don't worry about Swayne, Grump; we've got him tied into it now."

They passed close to the darkened C Bar house without stopping; with the crew there to protect the women, it was unlikely that any harm could come to them. Reaching the road that ran south out of Nazareth, they increased their pace and did not swing out into the basin until they were within three miles of town.

Fences could not be avoided. Letting themselves through stock gates cost them precious minutes. They had just struck Frank Warren's range, when his hay and barns were put to the torch. Though the fire was a mile away, the hay burned so fiercely that night was turned into day as the flames leaped skyward. The marauders could be seen dashing back and forth across the yard, at the rear of the house, overturning wagons and wrecking the corrals.

Rainbow called on the men to spread out and hold their fire until they got near enough to make their shooting count. In a thin line they surged forward, the roaring of the fire covering their approach until they were within two hundred yards of the house.

The partners identified Ben Slade, and a moment or two later they saw Pete Cleary whip out from the rear of the barn. Even as Cleary screamed a warning, he flung up his rifle and fired. The basin men responded with a crackling blast, yelling like Indians as they dashed in.

Taken by surprise, but refusing to stampede, Slade and his gunmen dropped back at once, working their guns viciously. A slug struck John Calvin and wounded him so seriously that his rifle went flying from his hands and he had to clutch his saddle horn to keep from going down. The rest swept past him, unstoppable now. In that charge, at least one of Slade's men was struck. His horse bolted and dragged him fifty yards before his foot became disentangled from the stirrup.

The running fight continued savagely, the crashing gunfire making the night hideous, until Slade's gang poured through a cut they had made in Warren's fence. It enabled them to gain a few yards on their pursuers. Being familiar with the basin, they turned off to the left and avoided the last fence between them and the hill trail. Outnumbered, flight was their only thought now.

Unsuspicious of the trap they were in, they drove straight for where Buck and his party were waiting. The latter made the grievous mistake of firing too soon. Realizing that he was being squeezed between the two forces, Slade swung sharply to the north and led his men back across the basin.

"They'll drive into town and hit the stage road to Buffalo Lodge!" Grumpy screeched at Rip.

The tall man was grimly aware of that possibility. Detaching Matt and five others, he ordered them to avoid Nazareth and cut into the road several miles below town.

"You'll have to hurry!" he warned. "If they get past you, they're gone!"

To give Matt a better chance, he let Slade's crowd pull away, believing it would slow their mad flight. The stratagem worked. When Slade found the stage road blocked, he turned back into Nazareth, knowing some help could be found there in Swayne's guards.

Swayne had been aroused by the gunfire out in the basin, as had everyone in Nazareth. From his window on the second floor of the hotel he had seen his blacklegs race through town. Sensing defeat, he had gathered his guards about him. There was an old pool table in the office. He had it tipped over on its side and dragged up against the foot of the stairs, where it made an effective barricade. Those preparations had been barely completed, when another rush of madly driven horses caught his ear. The riders drew up at the door and were out of the saddle before he saw that it was Slade and his men.

"Put your horses in back and get in here, you damned fools!" Swayne thundered.

They were just in time. Hard on their heels, Rainbow and his party galloped into town.

"They're in the hotel!" Grumpy cried triumphantly. "We got 'em treed!"

Rip silenced him with a glance. "It's a little too soon to do any crowing! You men keep out of sight. They'll pick you off from those upper windows if you don't!"

Shots were fired from the hotel almost immediately. It occupied a corner position, fronting on the main thoroughfare and extending back on a side street to a dilapidated barn and carriage shed. Across the way on this side street stood a blacksmith shop, a small lumber yard, and a small building used for storing barbed wire and heavy ranch hardware.

The tall man waved his men back out of range. "Don't give them a chance to pick you off," he told them. "We'll have men enough here in a few minutes to take that place apart if we want to."

John Calvin wasn't the only man who had been hit. Four others had sustained painful, if not serious, wounds. The property damage the basin cowmen had suffered ran into the thousands of dollars. Slade had lost two men and had three wounded, not including himself; a slug had barely ticked the tip of his right ear.

Having been ordered to block escape by the stage road, Matt and his little group remained where they were until they caught the sound of gunfire in town and presumed there was fighting there. As they rode in from one direction, Buck and his party came in from another. They had found Calvin and brought him in. He was barely conscious and in extreme pain. Two men got him to the doctor at once.

When Rainbow had disposed his forces so as to block off any chance of escape from the hotel, Cameron, Buck, and he conferred at length. Buck was all for attacking at once and bringing the fight to a speedy conclusion.

"There can't be more'n fifteen of 'em forted up in there," he argued. "We can bust into the office, Rip. They can't stop us—"

"They'll stop some of us, Buck. They've got a man posted at every second-floor window. At that distance, they couldn't miss. Do as you insist, and that side street will be littered with dead men."

"We certainly don't have to be in a hurry about this," said Matt, siding with Rainbow. "Lin will be back in the morning. Maybe we better wait for him—"

"What the hell can Lin Messenger do that we can't?" Buck demanded stubbornly.

"He can deputize us," Rip told him. "When Swayne sees that he's up against the law instead of a mob, it'll make considerable difference to him."

Buck was finally won over. It was after one o'clock already. Every few minutes a shot came from one or another of the upper windows of the hotel. Across the main street, a man showed himself momentarily on the roof of the post office and drew a hot fire, half a dozen slugs spattering the metal cornice a few inches from where he lay.

That outburst was followed by an uneasy quiet that became ever more tense and electric as the minutes passed. When Rip looked at his watch again, it was coming on to three o'clock. Grumpy and he were stretched out behind the iron watering-trough in front of the courthouse, from where they commanded a view of the hotel.

A pony's swift running, as it moved along the stage road, caught their ear as they lay there. The little one half rose and flicked a glance at Rainbow. "Whoever this is, he's comin' fast," he muttered, a vague anxiety edging his gruffness.

"Yeh," the tall man answered on the same note. "We better stop him before he rides into this hornet's nest."

They dodged away from the trough and reached the shadows cast by the line of shade trees that paralleled the sidewalk without being fired on. Seeing the unknown rider racing toward them, they ran out into the road and stopped him. To their surprise, he proved to be Lin Messenger.

"What goes on here?" Lin jerked out, breathing as heavily as his exhausted mount.

"I can't give it all to you in a word or two," said Rainbow. "This much I can tell you—we've had Swayne and his bodyguards and gunmen penned up in the hotel for hours— We didn't expect to see you until the morning stage got in."

"That was my intention," Lin informed them. "I reached the Lodge this evening and went to the stage barn, thinking if any of the boys was around I might find out what had been happening in the basin. While I was there, Slim Moody, Lester Moss's barn boss, drove in to put up a team for the night. He had just brought down Swayne's lawyers. Between what he knew and what he'd overheard them saying, I decided to saddle a horse and head for Nazareth at once."

Crossing the courthouse lawn, they reached the rear of the jail. With the wall of the building to shield them, they moved along it until they were within a step or two of the front door. Lin pushed in first and the partners followed. The briefing they gave him left little to be said.

Filled with wonder, Lin said, "You should have been a military man, Rip; you'd have made a great tactician. You had some able assistants, of course—Grumpy here and Miss Seng—"

"And a tremendous amount of luck," the tall man was quick to add. "My scheme could have backfired very easily. But there's no need to go into that; you're taking over now. There's enough authority in your badge to wind this thing up without too much trouble. I thought if you deputized all of us—"

"That'll be my first move." In the darkness of the office, a new soberness sounded in Lin's voice. It was as though he had suddenly grown older and wiser. "What did that gang do with their horses?"

"They're in the hotel barn."

"We'll rip a board or two off the back of the barn and lead the horses out. It'll leave that crowd high and dry." The sheriff unlocked a closet and secured a rifle. "Have you any idea where I'll find Matt?"

"The last we saw of him, he was hid out with some men in that little lumber yard across from the hotel," Rainbow told him. "You want to be careful, getting around to him."

"I'll go down the alley as far as the restaurant and cross the street there. The two of you better come with me. We'll lift their horses and wait for daylight, then."

"That won't be long," Grumpy remarked. "The sun will be showin' in another hour."

By the time they got around to the lumber yard, all of the basin men knew Messenger was back. Matt had Frank Warren and two others with him. He told them to concentrate their attention on the rear windows of the hotel and break up any gunfire from there while the horses were being removed from the barn.

Swayne's men were watching the barn. When they heard an entrance being made in the rear, they knew what it meant. There was little they could do about it without killing their own horses. In desperation, they began spattering the roof of the barn with slugs, the warped shingles flying off at weird angles. Matt and the others concealed in the lumber yard soon drove them back from the windows.

With the coming of dawn, Lin gave the basin men the oath and swore them in. Tying a handkerchief on a stick, he signaled for a parley. When a bedsheet was waved from an upper window, he walked out into the middle of the street and stopped.

"You men are under arrest," he called out. "This is a sheriff's posse now. If you give yourselves up, you will not be molested. I want you to come out with your hands in the air. I'm going to give you ten minutes to think it over. If you're not out by then, I'll have the hotel burned."

Dropping back, he waited, watch in hand.

The ten minutes were up when the overturned pool table was pushed back from the bottom of the stairs and Swayne filed out with his men. The former was still a truculent, defiant figure, but without his lawyers and Ron Huggins to lean on, he was a beaten man.

Having given his word that the prisoners would not be harmed, Lin stepped out with Matt, Warren, and the partners and drove the crowd back.

Slade and Cleary stared openmouthed at Rip and the little one for a moment and then tried to dart back into the hotel. Grumpy stopped them at gun point.

"What did I tell you!" Cleary snarled at Slade. "I knew some damned smart gent from outside was bossin' this fight!"

"Thanks for the compliment, Pete," was Rainbow's grim rejoinder. "If Ben had been a little smarter and burned those envelopes we found in his office in Mustang Gap, we might not have been able to trace you to Buffalo Lodge and your friend Swayne."

Slade glared at him with eyes that were murderous.

"This ain't the end, Ripley! There'll be more to it than this!"

"Not much more, Ben. We're not interested in your part in what you've done here; Idaho has a previous claim on you. There's warrants out on both of you for murder. As soon as the governor of Montana signs the extradition papers, you'll be on your way back to Mustang Gap."

Swayne whirled around, his face an apoplectic hue. "Ripley?" he croaked. "Do you mean to tell me I been fighting you and your partner all this time?"

"Just long enough for us to pull the rug out from under you," the tall man replied. "You're through, Swayne. When you were blowing off in that Chinese restaurant last evening, we had a couple of witnesses there who'll swear to what they heard you say."

The Nazareth jail had been built to house a maximum of seven prisoners. With twice that number and more lodged there, the walls were figuratively bulging. Away from the jail, excitement began to abate as the morning grew older. The ranchers who had been burned out, were the first to leave town. Rip was anxious to get back to C Bar. Matt asked him and Grumpy to wait while he saw Milo Sweet, the county attorney, and arranged with him to accompany them to the ranch so that he might get the sworn statements of Mei-lang and Cheng.

While waiting, encouraging word came of John Calvin's condition. He had been put to bed at the doctor's house and it appeared that he had a good chance of recovering.

Lin came up the street and insisted on the partners having a cup of coffee with him in Johnny's place.

"I've got Sam on the job, along with Herb Baker, another good man," he told them. "Swayne's hollering for a lawyer. He can holler. Nobody's putting his nose in that jail till the judge gets back. I suppose you fellows will be leaving the basin as soon as you can."

"We'll have to, Lin," said Rainbow. "Grump's going down to Buffalo Lodge on the noon stage and get some wires off that will start the wheels turning. It may be ten days or more before Slade and Cleary are taken off your hands. I'm waiting for Matt now. He's getting the prosecutor to go up with us. If we can make it, Mei-lang and Cheng and I will take the night stage out."

Lin stirred his coffee thoughtfully. "We folks around here owe the two of you a debt we'll never be able to repay."

"Forgit it," Grumpy told him. "We're even Stephen on that score. We couldn't have grabbed the men we wanted if we'd played it any other way."

The following afternoon in Billings, the partners and Cheng said farewell to Mei-lang. By taking the Northern Pacific to Seattle and going down the Coast, she could save a day in returning to San Francisco. Rainbow had a minute or two alone with her on the depot platform.

"It's hard to believe you are the same person Nazareth got used to seeing in Johnny Wong's place," he said admiringly.

She laughed softly. "I scandalized the Wongs by sitting up there in front, exhibiting myself to so many men. Rainbow, you are returning to Mustang Gap, but you will not be there long—"

"No, we'll wind up our job with the Denver and Pacific and head back to Wyoming."

"You could run down to San Francisco for a few days, first—couldn't you?"

The train rolled in, but he neither saw nor heard it.

"Would it mean so much to you, Mei-lang?"

"Everything, my darling!"

"And it won't keep you from coming to the ranch in the autumn?"

"No."

"On those terms, I'll come," he said, his voice husky with emotion.

She came close to him and felt his arms about her.

"Cheng is looking this way," she whispered, "but I can't help it—I've got to kiss you good-by."

The train was gone then, carrying her away.

"Wal, come on," Grumpy scolded, aware of what the

moment meant but taking that way of dulling its edge, "we've got a train to make, too. The sun's still shinin', Rip."

"I suppose it is," the tall man murmured disconsolately; "but not for me—right now."